The
Of The Innocents

In the *Valle de los Ingenios*, Cuba
(The Valley of the Sugar Mills)

Leonard Flama

ACKNOWLEDGMENT

Excerpt from *Fidel Castro* by Robert E. Quirk (1995) reproduced by kind permission of the publisher, W. W. Norton & Co. Inc.

ISBN: 978-1-326-83840-9

PublishNation
www.publishnation.co.uk

DEDICATION

This book is dedicated to Guillermina, Lorena, Zeida and the peopl of the *Valle de los Ingenios*, Cuba.

All proceeds from the sale of this book will be used to help th people of the Valle.

CONTENTS

Introduction

INTRODUCTION

In February 2006 I visited Cuba with my friend and fellow artist, Don Mead. We arrived at Varadero Airport at about three o'clock in the afternoon, and drove our hired car to the Hotel Oasis which was situated in the older, less touristic part of the town of Varadero. After a pleasant dinner accompanied with music by a live band, I went to bed at about midnight. The hotel was situated directly on the beach. I could hear the constant roar of the sea and thought that I would not be able to sleep that night. But I was tired from my travelling and sleep came fast. Before I knew it, I was awake again at six the next morning.

I had set my mental alarm clock to wake me early and my mind had selected 6:00 a.m. as the hour of rising in order to catch the sun as it came up over the horizon. I immediately got dressed and walked to the beach with my easel and painting materials. It was still dark at that hour of the morning and for a visitor to Cuba to get up so early was unthinkable. But the sun waits on no man, and I had to hurry in order to capture the first rays of sunlight as it came over the horizon and brightened up the fading night.

I was early and sat on the concrete jetty that protruded from the beach into the sea. This jetty was a monument now to past times and had withstood the relentless hammering of the waves. Sea moss was growing on it and a variety of baby sea crabs ran all over it and used it as their playground. I was alone, except for these sea crabs. Seagulls were notably absent, and it would seem that the morning was still too dark for them to come out in search of an early breakfast. It also seemed that they were not interested in seeing the sun rise that morning; they may have thought that they could see it rise on any morning of their choosing or that I, an intruder, had trespassed on their playground and prevented them from doing so.

However, I did not have to wait long for the sun. The dark sky gradually began to turn a subtle hue of orange and then into a creamy lemon, greyish, blueish colour which gave definition to the landscape and the tranquil constant sea. At this stage, the sea appeared a silvery grey and white as the waves rolled up to reveal the early brown of the beach. The sunrise came fast and lit up the sea and the land so that everything which had been in darkness a few seconds ago could be identified with the naked eye. As a result, I was only able to capture a few rough sketches of this sunrise. The sun must rise, the day must begin and time must make progress in the cycle of life, at whatever stage one decides to intervene. I was too slow to capture the rapidly changing colours in the various stages of their beauty.

I sat on the concrete pier for a few minutes after the sun had made its appearance, contemplating the spectacle of the colours which I had just seen. Unknown to me, Don had also risen early and was observing and photographing the sunrise from the beach some distance behind me. He, too, had seen the changing colours on the waters and was struck by their brilliance as night became day.

We were in Cuba and we considered this our first and profound impression of the island, as the evening before was short and we had not ventured out to see the sights and other attractions. Our journey would take us from Varadero to Santiago de Cuba and then back to Havana in the space of two weeks. I could describe the magnificent and interesting scenes which we encountered and the many people whom we met during the course of our journey – places such as Cardenas, Santa Clara, Sancti Spiritus, Las Tunas, Santiago, Camaguey, Trinidad, Cienfuegos and Havana, in chronological order of our travels. All had their uniqueness, and if I were to write at any length about them this introduction would end up in the making of another book of a thousand pages. That revelation would have to be for another time.

But if I had not encountered two little girls in the Valle de los Ingenios, near Trinidad, on our way back from Santiago, this introduction would have been for quite a different story – perhaps a travelogue on Cuba. But many writers have exhausted that genre in splendid fashion. The latest I have read was *The Island that Dared* by the renowned travel writer, Dervla Murphy.

The Valle de los Ingenios is located about twelve kilometres north-east from Trinidad. As we approached this intriguing historical site we saw a sign '*Welcome to the Valle de los Ingenios*' written large as we drove along the main *Carretera* road. We turned right into the road leading to the Valle and immediately saw the Manaca Mansion House and the Iznaga Tower which were situated at the end of a cobble-stone drive. The drive was lined by old wooden houses, which we later learned were some of the houses where the former slaves of the Valle lived. There were white sheets fluttering in the wind, apparently hung out to dry below the Tower, and people selling trinkets to the tourists who were visiting there in numbers.

After viewing the Mansion House and the Iznaga Tower for several minutes, I told Don that I would like to see more of the place and set off alone down the Lane (a dirt track) behind the Tower. That area, I felt sure, was prohibited to tourists but I managed to bypass the local residents, who would have known an intruder as soon as they saw one. I acted as if I was a Cuban – knowledgeable of the area and with business-like confidence and I was not questioned by anyone.

The Lane was leafy, punctuated by trees and shrubbery, and appeared desolate with no one in sight except two little girls who greeted me. I am sure they were shocked to see a stranger among them in their private residential surroundings. They were about five and seven years old and both of them had beautiful smiles. I thought the Lane was a lonely and desolate place for them to be – not knowing at the time that families were, in fact, living in every hut even though they were nowhere to be seen.

The two girls looked at me curiously as I spoke to them for a while in my broken Spanish. They laughed and appeared happy but I thought, on first impression, in this seemingly ideal place of a quiet life, that they were two angels who had found themselves in hell. My quick observation revealed that all the huts were dilapidated and looked to have been in that condition since the day they were built. I gave the girls a few pens and pencils and two cakes of Palmolive soap. The travel guides had advised me to go armed with such practical gifts. But the system in Cuba at that time was such that the local population was not encouraged to communicate or form relationships with foreigners, and that would apply especially to the residents of the Valle.

A woman came out onto the veranda of one of the huts to observe the 'stranger' who was speaking to the two girls. One of the girls said

3

that was her mother, and the woman said '*Buenos dias*' to me. I answered and went over and gave her two more cakes of soap for which she thanked me and, smiling, added something in Spanish which I did not understand. I took my leave of her and went further down the Lane, followed by the two girls. They all seemed to be of mixed blood and this was a surprise to me, for I was expecting to see the descendants of black African slaves. When I saw this, I wondered whether there were people of African descent still living in the Valle, or had they all moved away from the stigma of the place. Then I remembered that the people selling the trinkets to the tourists near the Tower were mainly black. The community, it seemed, had developed into a mixed society and I did not know to what extent that development had taken.

As I walked down the Lane, I came upon another hut where there appeared to be an elderly lady inside. I stopped and curiously looked into her house. She saw me and came out to greet me in the most friendly manner I had so far encountered on my journey around the island. I greeted her with '*Buenos dias*' and she replied with a gentle smile, standing barefoot on the dirt path leading to her house. She was a wrinkled meagre woman, with most of her bones showing as if she had not eaten for several weeks. The girls were still tagging along and, when I was invited by the lady to visit the inside of her house, they followed me and said that she was their grandmother. I then came to the conclusion that the two girls were sisters.

Inside the hut, my curiosity was assaulted by the conditions in which this lady was living. The hut was a one-room dwelling with a mud floor and sparse furniture that had long gone out of fashion in a disused junk-yard. She showed me her 'kitchen' which was separate from the hut. This was also primitive, and I quickly realised that she did not live there alone but shared her accommodation with the rats, insects, forest-worms and any wild creatures that resided in the vicinity and happened to smell whatever she was cooking at the time on her makeshift stone-constructed fire. There were holes in the roof and walls which were made of galvanised iron sheets that let in the bright sunlight and every known or unknown living creature that crawled among the undergrowth that scented her cooking whenever she was lucky to engage in such activity.

When I was leaving, I gave her a gift and thanked her for showing me around her hut – her private and personal living quarters which a stranger would not expect to see on first acquaintance. I sensed that she felt I was *simpatico* to her situation. She looked at me with such piercing eyes and detected that she was not wrong. I was moved by the occasion and the meeting with the two girls who seemed all alone in a deserted place except for their mother and grandmother.

On returning to the Mansion House, I sat outside observing the activities of the tourists and the local people who were allowed to sell their trinkets there. I looked at the Mansion House and the Tower and thought: 'Why do they still preserve and maintain this Tower of Torment after such a disreputable history?' I even went so far as to suggest to some of the locals that the Tower should have been demolished years ago as the sight of it was offensive. They laughed and may have thought that I was mad to have made such a suggestion.

It was only later that I realised that the Mansion House and the Tower were considered historical monuments and served as money earners for the government, as well as being a source of income for the residents of the Valle – one of the few opportunities for them to make a living which they would not otherwise have had. In the circumstances of their dire economy, they would have been worse off by its absence. UNESCO has granted World Heritage Site status to the Valle de los Ingenios. This signified to me that 'the Wind of Change' has blown over the Valle, and it is ironic that this heritage should be considered to have some degree of dignity.

I felt a little ashamed to have suggested that the Tower should be demolished and so deprive the residents from making a living. But I still felt uneasy about the Tower and the conditions of life of the people. I was not happy to be there as I felt that the Tower personally offended me.

As I finally departed from the Manaca Iznaga Estate, the encounter with the two little girls and their grandmother had left a profound impression on my mind. Yes, I had the strongest feeling that I would see them again, despite my reservations about the Tower.

We left the Valle and drove to our next stopover in Trinidad, en route to Havana where we spent a few days before returning to England. That was in 2006.

I was determined to learn more about the Valle de los Ingenios and read books on the subject and about Cuba generally. Within the next two years, I drafted my story on the Valle. I made it a fictional story, but a story mixed with fact, because I realised that my first visit to the Valle was a short one and that I had not had enough time to develop the facts about the people, their relationship with the government, their needs and expectations. I based my story on the two little girls as I saw them at the time – lonely, having only themselves for company, with a grandmother who, judging by her appearance, had suffered the ravages of life.

But time passed quickly and it was inevitable that I would return to the Valle de los Ingenios, which I did in February 2009, just days after Barack Obama was first inaugurated as President of the United States. I was to receive a different experience then, but by that time, I had already written the final chapters of my story.

The encounters of my subsequent visits to the Valle de los Ingenios are therefore left for another time when I am sure the story will be continued, God willing.

My comments on the politics of Cuba should be taken in the context of this fictitious story, and where the facts seem close to reality, that should also be taken as the result of an inventive imagination which could be either true or false. I have taken the liberty of making many assumptions and intelligent guesses in order to make my characters credible and believable.

Leonard Flama (2016)

CHAPTER ONE

THE VALLE

A cock crowed and Etna and Candelaria, two young sisters aged five and seven, knew that they had to wake from their slumbers. It was six o'clock in the morning and they had to rise and attend to Dulcina's demands – their precocious male fowl that had no respect for anyone, especially in the quiet of the mornings when dreams were being made in the little community in the Valle de los Ingenios, a place where former African slaves had laboured in the fields and in the sugar-mills in times past. The Valle is still, to some extent, worked for sugar-cane and there still exist the original slave huts which are occupied by the descendants of the slaves.

Dulcina was, of course, a feminine name but he was given the name 'Dulcina' because the other birds and animals were feminine and for the joys and simple pleasures that he brought to the two young girls' lives. He was a bright cherry-brown and black feathered bird which made his presence felt and exhibited himself at every opportunity to be admired by every other living creature in the Valle. He was undiplomatic and discretion was not part of his character. So, for his own good, he had to be caged along with the other birds and animals.

Yes, Dulcina was confident and may have acquired his extrovert attitude having survived five months with the girls' family. He had survived hard times and avoided the knife – when birds of his feathers were readily, and of necessity, despatched to the dinner table by their owners or the net of desperate hungry intruders who could not fail to be aware of his presence in the Valle. Such predators sharpened their knives many times, yet he survived.

Since times were hard, no day passed when even the rodents knew that they did not stand a chance for survival in the Valle for very long. So they learned quickly, became smarter and knew how to conduct themselves on the island in a period of chance.

Dulcina was alone now since his loving partner had not survived the demands of the times – the hungry bellies of its master had to be filled, and so they exercised the power of life and death. Even so, it was a lucky break for Dulcina, being born on the preferred side of the gender line – born a cockerel, he was not the first choice for the dinner table. Dulcina therefore believed that he could crow as loud as he pleased, without fear, and it did not matter that he did not hear an echo of his call, for there were no others like him to be found in the Valle. They had suffered the ultimate sanction of their existence in this time and place.

The girls had to get up and also attend to the surviving chicks – four in number - and a young goat that was given to them by their uncle, Silvio. They would dress themselves, and then walk to the back of the house and feed Dulcina, the chicks and the kid-goat. This goat was young but wise enough to provide just sufficient milk to remain important to the family.

Dulcina would observe this activity and would have been aware that he was not making a contribution and that his presence was noisy and unproductive. Fortunately, he had the affection of the girls, and that saved him from the dinner table. The girls would stroke his head and caress his plumes and he felt reassured. The girls loved that bird.

They also talked to the young chicks and asked them in turn what they wanted to be when they grew up. The girls would have liked to have saved them from the dinner table if they could, but knew that their time of tears would come sooner than they would have wished. But for now they did not think of it and enjoyed the company of their 'friends' which broke the solitude of their existence and make them forget their meagre way of life in the Valle.

'How are you today, Nanny-goat?' they would ask, and pause a while as if expecting her to answer. 'I am in good health and have lots of milk for you today,' she would seem to imply. The girls knew a healthy animal by the sound of its bleating and the shine of its silvery coat. This goat was a comparative newcomer to the den, but she seemed to know how to act appropriately and how to please. She had arrived in the Valle three weeks before and would have observed the antics of Dulcina and the favourable treatment he received.

'We shall now name you 'Gallina' (Hen) because we are all female chicks here and since Dulcina does not have a playmate, except these small chicks, you will have to be his playmate.'

Gallina, the goat, bleated and showed her teeth in agreement. But Gallina did not want to be called a 'Hen'. She was most definitely a beast of the animal species, but she was wise not to display any objection to being called a 'Hen'. If the girls loved her and they were happy to call her 'Gallina', she was not going to display any tantrums because she knew that if she was favoured by the girls, she would survive any sudden unforeseen demand or change of diet of the family. 'They can call me 'Gallina' or 'Hen' or whatever name they wish; I will remain obedient and as pleasant as the gentle breeze that cools these early mornings in the Valle – although my genes are those of the *Cabra* family, proud beasts that we are,' Gallina would have thought.

It was time for breakfast and the girls received the call: 'Etna, Candelaria, it's time for breakfast', announced Amelia, their mother. It was a proud declaration made by a mother who had something to place before her daughters. Etna was seven and Candelaria just five, but they knew the significance of breakfast time. They knew that whatever their mother had prepared for breakfast would be nourishing, but that it also would be in short supply. There was no need to rush to the table only to excite their stomachs to expect more than was available. Since they did not expect it at breakfast time, they certainly did not expect it at lunch or dinner time and therefore they were not disappointed.

The girls would have preferred to remain speaking to their feathered friends and to Gallina. They thought of them as personal friends and dealt with them as individuals. Each one had its own personality, character and special mannerisms. They saw so much more in these creatures than they saw in humans. They spoke their language, loved and cared for them more than human beings, except their parents, and were appreciated by them. How this affinity to living creatures and the natural world came about could not be explained by their parents. The environment in which they lived, and the solitude of that environment, may have had something to do with it.

There were other children of similar ages who lived in some of the nearby huts, but more often than not Etna and Candelaria were seen by themselves speaking to the wild birds and other creatures which inhabited their mini-forest. The birds would sit on their heads and on their shoulders and the wild animals would eat from their hands as if they were all trained in the art of friendship. Their neighbours and other human friends must have thought them odd for choosing to be alone with their wild friends in preference to their peers and school friends. But the girls were happy and considerate and were loved by all who lived in the Valle.

As the girls walked back towards their house for breakfast, Dulcina began to crow. He had eaten up all the feed which the girls had provided for him. He was always a greedy bird and did not realise how lucky he was to have sympathetic providers who would do their very best to make sure that he was well fed, even if the girls did not have much to eat for themselves.

The girls were getting up earlier and earlier because Dulcina decided to commence crowing long before the sun showed any signs of rising over the horizon. He increasingly deprived the girls of their sleep and was making a fool of himself in the eyes of their parents and all the people in the Valle who could not avoid hearing him at that early hour of the morning. Dulcina did not realise that he was a risk-taker, for at any time his neck could have been cut to silence him or to quench an unsympathetic listener's hunger. But he survived because everyone in the Valle knew that he was the loving pet of Etna and Candelaria.

The girls crossed their small garden of parched earth, numbed by the heat of the sun, to their house. There was no moisture in this area of soil and the earth flaked and created a wind of dust which became more irritating in the summer. Nothing grew in this plot because the land had either been over-worked in the past or the water level was diverted elsewhere. It was only in the rainy season that this plot's thirst was quenched and the soil became suitable for planting. But soon after, the hurricanes would come and destroy everything in sight that was not battened down, especially the gentle plants and trees.

The Martinez family was unfortunate because just a few metres from their house the grass was green and the beginning of the mini-forest commenced. It seemed as if they were singled out to experience even greater hardships than their neighbours, for they too were experiencing hard times.

Both girls were slim due to their diet or, rather, lack of diet. They loved each other and, when they were not speaking to the birds, they chatted to each other and were each other's best friends. They never quarrelled, kept each other's secrets, if there were any, and were always truthful to their parents.

After washing their hands at the external water pipe, the girls entered their mother's kitchen – made of wood and galvanised iron sheets. The sound of running water attracted passing wild birds and made them vulnerable to human predators who did not have the special affinity to wild creatures which the girls possessed. These wild inquisitive birds needed to be more alert, but they could be forgiven for not being aware that the predators in the Valle were hungrier and more demanding.

'Has Papa gone to work already?' asked Candelaria.

'Yes, he could not wait for you,' said Amelia.

'What are we having for breakfast today?' asked Etna.

'We are having the last of my baked coconut bread and some papaya fruit,' said Amelia.

'But we had that yesterday, Mama,' said Candelaria.

'And you may have it again tomorrow and the rest of the week,' said Amelia.

'Can we have some meat for dinner then?' asked Etna.

'It's a lucky thing that your Papa is not here to have heard what you said,' said Amelia. 'If you love those chicks as much as you do, you had better mind what you say, and be thankful what God has placed before you.'

'Papa would not dare touch those little chicks. We have not even given them their names as yet,' said Etna.

'Then don't complain for something other than what is on the table,' said Amelia, in a stern voice, trying to make them realistic about their dire circumstances.

'Dulcina is …' Candelaria was about to say something.

'Don't say it. I know exactly what you are about to say: That that cock is still hungry. He can crow as much as he wants, he is not going to get any more food until tonight. He eats more than we do!' said Amelia.

Their mother was absolutely right to point out the enormous appetite of Dulcina. She knew that if she did not keep a watchful eye on the two girls they would salvage most of their food for their feathered friends and that conniving Gallina, leaving little for themselves. And after breakfast, even after their mother had spoken, that was exactly what the girls did – their mother's coconut bread was secreted under the table destined for the birds and the goat.

This was the game they played every day. Amelia cautioned and the girls, by sleight of hand, bolted their food. They seemed to be firm in their belief that if they did not have sufficient to eat themselves, their 'friends' should not suffer as well.

The girls were not only concerned about their immediate feathered friends. They were also concerned about the other wild birds that passed their way, such as the *Cartacuba* with its white, orange and blue plumage, the *Tocororo* with its distinctive red, white and blue plumage, or the tiny *Zunzuncito* with black and brilliant emerald green feathers on its way to the swamp lands.

These birds were also attracted by the feeding of Dulcina and the chicks. There was no competition because these wild birds were birds of passage – here today and gone today because they could not wait until tomorrow to eat. But while they sojourned in the Valle they were greatly admired and appreciated. The girls would spend hours observing their behaviour, mannerisms and all their antics as they descended upon the few pieces of bread fed to them - their alertness, nervousness and constant apprehension of attack upon their fragile nature before they could commence eating. Every alert radar with which they were equipped was poised to avoid intrusion or capture.

'Do not play far today,' said Amelia, after the girls had washed and dressed.

'No Mama, we will only go down the Lane as far as Grandma and the rail-track,' said Etna. It was Saturday, and the girls had all day to play and to investigate their surroundings in minute detail.

The Lane was the playground of the innocent – their innocence. It was a grassy dirt track that gradually sloped down into the Valle. The underground water seemed to nourish more the soil there. It was surrounded by a few fruit trees and green bushes and was a safe haven for a variety of birds, lizards and small insects. The track was known as 'the Lane'.

At first, there seemed to be no activity along the Lane, except for the wild creatures. It seemed a desolate and lonely place – a private wild garden where only the girls and their feathered friends and animals roamed. But there were other houses of similar construction to theirs dotted around this semi-forest hideaway. They were all neighbours known to one another and their children also attended the same school as Etna and Candelaria. But today they were all inside their homes which made the Valle quieter than usual.

Their grandmother's name was Mabelina. She lived only a few metres down the Lane, but the girls would dawdle for hours before they could reach her house – usually their ultimate destination. It was not unknown for the girls to have taken two or three hours to get there. The usual array of assorted birds and insects that frequented the lush vegetation and also other numerous attractions absorbed their young and inquisitive minds, causing them to linger and investigate. The sight of a pygmy owl which decided to rest in the trees for a few hours, or the multi-coloured butterflies that breached the monotony of the greenery and added colour to the environment, or the girls' pursuit of a wild creature as it disappeared into the undergrowth may have been responsible for the length of time it often took` them to reach Mabelina's house.

On this occasion, when they eventually arrived at the bottom of the Lane, they walked past Mabelina's house. They could see her busy inside, cleaning. They did not need to call out to her because she had already seen them as they approached the house. Their sudden appearance was no surprise to her because it was the girls' usual habit to visit her every day, whenever they felt like doing so, unannounced nor by appointment.

To them, Mabelina's house was like an extended room of their parents' house. What difference did it make if it was a few metres down the Lane, and – when the bushes were overgrown – they could not be seen? The girls were perfectly safe and at home.

A few metres' walk further down the Lane, they reached the defunct rail-track that curved from west to east and was now overgrown with wild grass and flowers. It was a single track that had been used in the past to transport the sugar-cane and agricultural products from deeper into the Valle de los Ingenios. It was with mixed feelings that one looked upon this sight – to see its discarded remains which hid the fractured space of activity and the forced labour that had contributed its cargo and operated its wheels in former times.

Of course, Etna and Candelaria did not know the history of the environment in which they lived. They were too young to have been formally instructed in such matters but, through overheard conversations of their parents and their friends, they acquired all sorts of information on a variety of subjects and were learning fast.

The girls learnt that the metal track was not built for the horse and cart and wondered why they did not see a railway locomotive in operation. They knew what a railway locomotive was because they had travelled on a train before, when they visited the nearest town of Trinidad, about twelve kilometres away. Such travel would have been an exceptional adventure for them and one which they certainly would have remembered – the shaking, rattling, rolling and the black smoke from the wood fuel that propelled the steam engine along the wider extent of the Valle. The experience would have taught them that they were living in a beautiful place with an interesting history which they could not imagine in their innocent minds.

Across the rail-track, in the immediate vicinity of Mabelina's house, there were three other houses a few metres apart. The people who lived there were good neighbours.

Today, they all seemed to be away – men and women working in the fields. Or perhaps some of the women were busy at home, embroidering tablecloths and other linen items for sale, and the children who lived there were assisting their parents in this activity. As a result, the Lane seemed more isolated and lonely than usual, except for Etna and Candelaria who had their special 'friends' to play with and to speak to – lively conversations and the conduct of classes with them, as if the Lane was filled with chattering human activity.

'Should we go and see Lucia and Magenta, and ask them to come out to play with us?' asked Candelaria.

'You know that they would not be allowed to. They have to help their mother,' said Etna.

'But why do they have to help their mother? They are only children like us.'

'Mama said that they have to make some pesos because their father does not live with them any more,' said Etna.

'Would our Papa stop living with us, Etna?'

'Our Papa loves Mama too much to do that.'

'Doesn't Papa love us also?' asked Candelaria.

'You know he does,' said Etna.

'Yes, and so do our 'friends' and we would not leave them and go away, would we, Etna? ' said Candelaria.

It was a rhetorical question to which Etna did not have to give an answer. Instead she gave her sister a curious look which suggested that she should not ask such foolish questions since their 'friends' were the most important things in their lives apart from their parents.

Eventually, it was time to visit Mabelina and to spend some time with her and talk about the things she was going to do that day. Their enquiry would have been more pertinent three hours earlier, but since they had taken so long to get to her house the question seemed to have lost its relevance. But, for the girls, time was not important. They were growing up into the slow and casual pace which was now the accepted mode of life in the Valle. They stopped and looked back in the direction from where they had come, and saw the Iznaga Tower. It cast a shadow of a giant man armed with hammer and nails, poised to drive them into the soil.

Today's residents of the Valle sell trinkets to the tourists and seem happy that the Tower draws these to a place where they can do a little business and earn themselves some money – money which goes a long way in the present economic climate, especially if the prices are paid in dollars or convertible pesos. The residents are richer by the dozen for they seem to be benefiting from the blood of their ancestors and the remnants of the Valle's ignoble monuments.

Etna and Candelaria would not have had knowledge of these matters, and they were prohibited from the area around the Manaca Mansion House. Their world was the Lane and the immediate neighbours around them. They went to visit their grandmother, Mabelina. She lived alone in one of the former slave huts near the rail-track – the boundary of the girls' walk that day.

Mabelina was a woman who was perhaps only about sixty years old, although she looked more like eighty. She was slim – too slim for her age and the size of her bones. She certainly looked under-nourished. She had a kind and friendly face, but a face marked by the ravages of hard times spent on the wrong side of poverty. Every crease on her face could have represented ten years and she had so many creases that she could have been ninety years old. But she was a kind woman, always ready with a smile and to be helpful to others. She bore her hardships without complaint.

She lived in a one-room wooden hut with an external kitchen, in conditions not much different from the austerity of the slave. Her single bed, made of wire, was screened by an embroidered patchwork sheet in order to provide some degree of privacy from the few immediate neighbours who lived in the shadow of the Tower or from the unexpected official who may have come to establish that she was still alive. Her house did not possess a single modern item of convenience. She was a forgotten citizen of the Revolution.

Mabelina's kitchen annex was a small room with a dirt floor, and her cooking facility was located in a corner of that floor – made of stones placed together and wood from the mini-forest which surrounded her hut. Her cooking equipment was equivalent to that of a gold prospector in the days when that valuable material was first discovered and men lived rough. But even though she lived in a dilapidated house with a dirt floor, she still dusted every day and tried to keep her living accommodation clean – knowing that she would always lose the battle.

Mabelina was kind and loving to Etna and Candelaria. She was a second mother to them. Her activities were usually in and around the house, on her own energy, still determined to be independent. But these characteristics were no surprise to those who knew her well.

Mabelina had been married to Jorge Martinez whom she had known since childhood. They were neighbours since Jorge's father had bought his farm in Camaguey. They attended the same school and grew up within sight of each other. It seemed inevitable to both families that Jorge and Mabelina would get married to each other, and they did so when they were of age.

Jorge was a good husband and a gentleman. His formal education was brief, having, as a young boy, worked with his father in the big estates which were owned by the Americans who had a monopoly. He learned his farming from them. He was a pragmatist, realising that there was money to be made in the farming business for one who was willing to work hard. But he was not over-ambitious and kept his farm at a size that was manageable by two workers and himself.

When the Revolution came, Jorge supported it because he believed that the agricultural monopolies would be redistributed and controlled and the smaller farmers would have a better chance of competing. Jorge continued to work hard believing that he would be rewarded for his hard work.

When his two sons, Cardenzo and Silvio, were born within two years of each other, he promised Mabelina that he would make sure that they got a good education so that they could manage the farm on his retirement. But, as the boys were growing up, they both opted to work on the farm. Perhaps they thought that further education would have been too expensive for their parents to afford. They may also have observed that their parents were working all hours on the farm. So when both sons told their father that they wanted to work full time on the farm, he was disappointed but did not object too strongly. He knew that the farm was for the mutual benefit of all the family and Cardenzo and Silvio would share their inheritance.

The Martinez family could not compete with the bigger farms which specialised in the planting and harvesting of sugar-cane and the manufacture of sugar and its by-products. So Jorge and his sons concentrated on the production of cash-crops: bananas, other fruits and tobacco.

By then, the future was mapped out for Cardenzo and Silvio. Jorge believed that when his sons got married they would live with their wives on the farm and continue the business as a joint enterprise. When either of their parents died, their sons would care for the one who survived. Both sons accepted this arrangement.

But Jorge's sons were different in character. Cardenzo was reserved and more like his father, and was ready to accept all his ideas in relation to the farm. Silvio was a reluctant participant. He wanted more from life than mere survival. He disputed most of his father's ideas and instructions and suggested his own. If something was wrong, Silvio would openly speak about it, whether it caused offence or not. Cardenzo was just the opposite. Silvio was more adventurous and ready to argue his point of view with his father but, in the end, he had to capitulate for the peace and proper management of the farm. Both sons loved their parents and each other dearly.

Cardenzo and Silvio did, however, have certain things in common. They were of mixed blood – African and Spanish. As a result, they suffered the consequences of not being full-blooded Spanish. Contentions came to a head throughout their school life and always resulted in fights, with Silvio taking the initiative in defending his honour. Cardenzo may have been reluctant to initiate such battles but he participated in support of his brother.

They were neither white nor black. They considered themselves 'in-betweens', open to ridicule and resentment. They knew that the majority of the population were of Spanish blood and still looked to Spain as the 'motherland', although its political control and responsibility had been over for many years. They disliked hearing people say that their ancestors were from Sevilla or Galicia or Tenerife. Such statements imply a recognition of the differences among the races and set in motion class bias and conflicts. Silvio particularly resented that greatly.

Both brothers did not care who ruled the island, as the rulers were always of Spanish descent. Fidel Castro was of that mould. The Revolution was supposed to work for the benefit of all the people but its policies did not work out that way. The hopeful years which their father, Jorge, had expected were quickly dashed, and stringent rules and regulations with a strict adherence to Socialism were put into place.

The Martinez family still fought to overcome any difficulties which tried to hinder them from maintaining their farm and their reasonable standard of living. But one day, when they received a Notice from the Department of Agriculture and Lands that their little farm would be absorbed into a larger co-operative, they knew that it was the beginning of the end of their independence and their way of life in Camaguey. They could not fight against the acquisition because to do so would have been unsuccessful and they would have been accused of being traitors to the Revolution. Such was the mode and feeling at the time.

The family was relocated to the Valle de los Ingenios, to live and to work in the large plantations which were now controlled by the Revolutionary regime. Cardenzo accompanied his parents to the Valle, being the elder of their two sons and the one who felt that he had the greater responsibility for their welfare. Silvio no longer felt that commitment since the farm was acquired by the Revolution. Being younger and more adventurous, he decided to go to Havana.

Jorge died soon after arriving in the Valle. He became depressed, believing that he had disappointed his wife and sons. Since he could not conform to the life in the Valle, his health gradually deteriorated – pining away for the good old days of their lives in Camaguey before the Revolution.

When Jorge died it was the saddest period of Mabelina's life, for he was not only her husband, but had also been her best friend since they were children.

Life in the Valle was not the same as living on their little farm in Camaguey where they had been masters of their own destiny. But change was forced upon them and Mabelina had to adapt. She quickly became the matriarch in the Valle's small community – respected by all and respecting all, for they were in the same boat of poverty.

'You must be hungry,' Mabelina said to Etna and Candelaria, as they went into her house.

'Yes, Grandma,' said both girls in unison. This was the normal procedure of their lives. Every day, Mabelina would ask the girls if they were hungry and they would answer: 'Yes, Grandma'. Mabelina knew their answer by now for she had been asking that question for most of their lives.

Mabelina's kitchen was already filled with smoke from the wood fire under the pot that cooked the meal of the day – papaya, sweet potatoes, plantain, mamey fruit and a portion of compressed meat loaf allocated from her rations. Most of the provisions were harvested from her back garden or from fruits growing wild in the surrounding mini-forest and, therefore, she usually had something to eat, depending on the seasons.

Fresh meat, as part of the menu, was a rarity, unless Mabelina was fortunate to have caught some hapless wild animal, such as a rabbit, in one of her traps or a wild bird which was so careless as to be caught. She would not have told Etna and Candelaria that such a catch was being served up for lunch. The girls lived too close to nature and considered themselves in fraternity with the wild birds and animals with which they conversed every day. Every bird was a 'Dulcina' and every wild animal was a 'Gallina'.

'What are you cooking today, Grandma?' asked Candelaria.

'Papaya and plantains - your favourites,' said Mabelina.

'We're sorry that we couldn't bring you some eggs. We do not have a hen to lay them,' said Etna.

'That's kind of you, Etna, but don't worry. I am sure that you will get a hen very soon,' said Mabelina.

'Papa said that there are no hens anywhere because the people have eaten them all up,' said Etna.

'And that we may not have hens any more, forever,' said Candelaria.

'I am sure there will be plenty of hens in the future. Remember that hens have wings and they can fly. They could fly from the country where they now live to our beautiful island,' said Mabelina, in an effort to console the girls. She could not tell them that their Papa was right. They were living in modern times and the economy of the island should have been a success story. Cuba was and had been living under an embargo for over 40 years. Although this was not the most difficult period of their Socialism, there were still many shortages and times were still hard for the people, and especially for those in the Valle.

'Have you finished the embroidery on the two dresses?' asked Etna.

'No, I'm still working on them. You know that I will sell them to the tourists when they are finished.'

'Can we see them?' asked Candelaria.

'Yes, they are on the bed. Open the blind. Are your hands clean?' asked Mabelina.

'We will wash them,' said Etna, and they went to the water pipe outside and washed their hands.

'Oh, they are lovely!' said Candelaria.

'And this one is just my size. I wish it was for me,' said Etna.

'Those are for sale. I shall make you a similar one another time. Put them away now, your meal is ready.'

Mabelina had to be honest and forthright with the girls because, if she was not, it would have been so easy to have given in to their pleadings for the dresses to be given to them as a gift. But she could not afford to do that. She had to have a means of survival, and the making and sale of the dresses was the only way she knew how to earn an income. She may have appeared to be wobbly on her feet and on her last legs of life, but the dexterity of her fingers in sewing and embroidering different types of garments showed that she still had the energy and capability of being independent.

The meal was served hot and it was no surprise to Mabelina that the girls enjoyed it. They were always hungry. Her old cooking pots and pans should have been replaced for new ones long ago, but they did not fail to produce the results that she wanted. She was affectionately attached to those pots and pans and would not have parted with them even if new ones were given to her. New ones cost money and she could not afford them. She had learnt many years ago not to desire the material things of life.

She was reconciled and content, so far as anyone could be content in her circumstances – a state of mind which must be quickly adopted when better cannot be done or the impossible achieved. This state of acceptance was made a little easier to achieve since all her neighbours and friends were in much the same boat. She made the maximum use of her two wooden chairs, her wire bed and her rocking-chair – all dating back to the 1940s – and her pots and pans which had survived the many occasions when they had been soldered to make them serviceable again.

It was three o'clock and time for the girls to leave Mabelina and make their short journey home – two skips up the dirt Lane at the back of the Iznaga Tower and they would be there. Although they had been away for several hours, their mother did not fear for their safety. They were obedient girls and their mother knew that she could rely on their honesty. But good parents always supervise their children, and so their mother always kept an eye on their movements, although she knew that her daughters were safe in the Valle.

And if, by chance, the girls were not where they were supposed to be, she was always informed by one of the neighbours where they could be found playing. The neighbour most aware of the girls' movements was 'Señor Green Tree'. He was also known as 'The Invisible Man' because of his green outfit which made him appear to merge almost invisibly into the foliage. He lived in one of the huts beyond the old locomotive rail-tracks, and every day he could be seen tending his garden when he was not roaming around the Valle with his machete.

Etna and Candelaria were not permitted to venture in the opposite direction beyond the Iznaga Tower. There was too much traffic of cars and people circulating there. They would be in danger of being injured by the big tourist buses, and the tourists were considered as strangers of different cultures. Their presence there may also have been prohibited by the Management of the Estate having a policy that residents who did not have any lawful business there should not frequent that area.

Those residents who sold trinkets and embroidered materials and other tourist souvenirs were permitted to ply their trade. They may have had special permission or been granted a licence to do so. Mabelina would have been one of them. This was an effective way for the authorities to keep control and collect a licence tax.

Etna and Candelaria did not know the reason why they were prohibited from that part of the Manaca Iznaga Estate. In fact, they did not know many things about the place in which they lived. Their parents, and more informed adults, may have thought that they were too young to understand the history of the Estate and the Valle, or that their childhood should not be tainted by unpleasant events which had taken place in the past but which had left a profound impact by the existence of the Manaca Mansion House, the Iznaga Tower and the all-absorbing nature of the Valle de los Ingenios.

'We had a nice day today with our friends', said Etna.

'Your school friends?' asked Amelia.

'No, Mama. They did not come out to play today,' said Etna.

'Oh, you mean the birds in the trees and the little creatures that live in the fields,' said Amelia.

'And with Grandma too,' said Candelaria.

'And did your 'friends' speak to you and sing for you?'

'You know they always do, Mama. They sing so sweetly. I wish I was a bird,' said Candelaria.

'Yes, not only to sing, but to fly from tree to tree, to see the world and to meet so many other friends,' said Etna.

'Did you give them names?' asked Amelia.

'No, they all seemed to be in a hurry to fly away. If they return tomorrow, we will give them names,' said Etna.

'But we have to name the chicks first,' said Candelaria.

'You can do that at feeding time. Right now, you must do a little of your school work.'

'But I am tired, Mama,' said Candelaria.

'I am too, Mama,' said Etna.

'All right, have a sleep for a little while, but when you get up, you must do some school work, OK?'

Etna and Candelaria went to their room and, within a few minutes, the house was quiet again for the two girls had fallen asleep. They would dream about the wild birds and animals, and when they awoke they would tell their mother all about their dreams and have animated discussions about what they were going to do the next day. They would do their school work, greet their Papa when he returned from work, feed the chicks and say goodnight to them and to Dulcina and Gallina, and, later, kiss their Papa and Mama goodnight. They would then go to bed, but before going to sleep they would read their story books about the elephants and tigers of Africa and India or the llamas of Peru. Gradually, their eyes would close and they would dream about those places and of birds and animals and the beauty of the world.

CHAPTER TWO

INFORMAL EDUCATION

At about seven o'clock the next morning, Etna and Candelaria were already awake and feeding Dulcina, Gallina and the chicks. It was the day that the chicks were to be named. For most of the night, the girls had thought about the names that they would give them and, by the time they went to sleep, they had agreed on what they would name them: 'Pinky', because its beak was almost coloured pink; 'Dotty', because that chick had a few black spots which gave it a strange appearance among its yellow plumes; 'Hungry', because that chick ate more than the other three and therefore was the fattest; and 'Tiny', which was the smallest of the family. 'Tiny' did not seem to be eating much, for it was deprived of its food by 'Hungry', and so it remained undernourished and lonely. There was much sympathy for 'Tiny' and the girls thought that they must do something about the problem. But at present they could not decide what to do. They would have to speak to their Papa about it.

After feeding the wild birds outside the enclosure, they lingered a while to observe the antics of a bird which was struggling with a worm too large to consume all at once. The bird played with it and tossed it about, and with every motion to subdue the worm, it went through its ritual of alertness, suspicion, nervousness and expectant attack by unseen predators. Finally, the worm was torn in half and the bird took one half in its beak and flew away, leaving the other half to be devoured by the first feathered competitor flying by or patiently waiting for most of the hard work to be done by the first bird. It would seem that birds have some common sense – bird sense – knowing when to be brave and stand their ground and also knowing when to take flight to other pastures or to wait for an opportune moment.

Etna and Candelaria were learning about life – natural life – the birds and animals and all that nature could provide in their immediate environment. They did not have to go in search of it. It came upon them, as they were part of the environment where constant exposure to it drew them closer to every living creature that could be found in their little world. They were very happy and did not know the evils of greed or avarice or cruelty or deception or a malicious feeling or thought. They seemed content with life, although they were born poor and had no other expectation but to grow up poor.

Etna was two years older than Candelaria but they were like twin sisters – both intelligent and learning from each other. They were in each other's company from morning until night. They discussed everything with each other and protected each other. They had loving parents who did not trouble their daughters' minds about politics, economics, the Revolution or the history of their island, especially concerning the place in which they were living and were happy. The girls were angels – among the few admirable and honourable things that existed in the Valle de los Ingenios.

But life is a continuous learning process – one can learn by express instruction or by self-application or by observation. Although the girls were too young to have certain information imparted by their parents or their school, they, nevertheless, obtained a lot of information, and therefore, indirectly, an informal education, by observation and from overhearing conversations engaged in by their parents, friends and neighbours.

One such occasion was on a visit of Señor and Señora Bronski, their neighbours who lived in one of the huts just beyond the rail-track. The girls would overhear certain conversations about the politics of their country and try to make sense of what was being discussed.

Señor Carlos Alvarez Bronski and Señora Caterina Bronski were good friends of the Martinez family. In fact, all the neighbours who resided in and around the area of the rail-track were good friends, trusted one another and would discuss all matters, including some that could be very delicate with a stranger.

'Did you hear that the Comandante fell down some steps the other day?' asked Bronski.

'No. What happened?' asked Cardenzo.

'They said that he was attending the Anniversary of the Revolution rally and, when he had finished his speech and was going down the steps of the building, he lost his balance and fell.'

'Did he hurt himself?' asked Cardenzo.

'Oh no, he just got up and walked on. But they said that he was shaken by the fall.'

'The Comandante is a very strong man. They cannot get rid of him so easily,' said Cardenzo.

'Some people thought, when they saw him fall, that they had tried again to assassinate him,' added Señora Bronski.

'If it was another assassination attempt, it would have been over 600 times that they have tried to kill him,' said Bronski.

'I believe that the more they try to assassinate him, the more they prove how important he is to Cuba,' said Cardenzo.

'Yes, the Comandante is important because he is successful and a survivor. Look at the progress we have made in the last few years,' said Bronski. 'If we could survive the 'Special Period' between 1989 and 1995, we can survive anything. My son, Augusto, was born just before then, and I was determined that he would grow up and make a name for himself.'

'How is Augusto doing in Havana?' asked Amelia.

'He seems to be doing very well at university, and we hope he will be a doctor in five years' time. Fortunately, education is now free to everyone,' said Señora Bronski.

'Only for the young. We didn't have the opportunity to take advantage of that. We still have to work in the farms or wherever we are directed by the Committee. Things have not improved for us – there are still shortages of many essential items,' said Cardenzo.

'That's life, Cardenzo. But you must admit that things have changed for the better. We have good health and education programmes, and our children – your daughters – will benefit from our labour and the hardships we suffer,' said Bronski.

'What will life be like when our two girls grow up? It may not be the same as we know it today. The Comandante and his brother may not be ruling the country. Would we return to capitalism? I am afraid for the future of our children because everything seems equal now but, later, greed and avarice will corrupt the minds of our people,' said Amelia.

'My wife is right. I know that you believe strongly in the Socialist system and its survival after the Comandante and Raul. I have spoken to others and I have overheard conversations reflecting the fears of many people. They do not dispute that the Revolution is successful and, if given a chance, it could be an even greater success. But they think that Cuba is very vulnerable because it is situated in the jaws of the tiger and the Americans will not rest until our island comes under their control again,' said Cardenzo.

'Yes, the Revolution is a success, but the senseless embargo which the Western countries impose upon Cuba is hampering our progress. The embargo should be removed to allow us to live our lives as free citizens – free to demand all that is expected of a free and independent nation,' said Bronski.

'But could we really be free in our country to live our lives as we want? Both our families have been sent to this Valle to cut sugar-cane and work on agricultural projects. I believe that we are capable of doing better for ourselves and our families, but we have no choice in the matter,' said Cardenzo, raising his voice a little from the subdued tones which they had adopted at the beginning of their conversation.

'Be careful not to speak too loudly, Cardenzo. Remember that there are ears of the Committee everywhere,' said Señora Bronski.

'You're right. I got carried away there for a moment. But you have just proved my point – that we do not have freedom of speech or action in our own country,' said Cardenzo.

'My friend, I fully understand what you say and empathise with you. There are many things in our country which could be improved and I, myself, would like to see those improvements sooner rather than later,' said Bronski.

'Now Carlos, you must admit that it was foolhardy of the Comandante to allow Russian missiles to be positioned on Cuban soil – given the Cold War which existed between the US and Russia at the time,' ventured Cardenzo.

'Since I am always honest with you, Cardenzo, I will admit that was foolhardy. Every nation has an inalienable right to take what actions they like concerning their own country, but when that right affects other people or other nations, they must think carefully whether they should exercise that right.'

'But wasn't it because of that mistake, that the embargo was imposed upon us which has caused our people to suffer for so many years?' asked Cardenzo.

'It's easy to say that but, if I am to be honest with you, I must say that was not the real reason for the embargo. Once the Russian missiles had been destroyed or removed from Cuban soil, there was no longer any threat. The viper's tooth given to the docile dog had been pulled.

Although the United States has officially prohibited its citizens from travelling to Cuba, they still visit here and we welcome them as friends. Some of them even display the American flag on their T-shirts without fear of resentment or of being challenged by our people or Government.

The true reason for the embargo was based on the differences in ideologies. But the question I want to ask you, Cardenzo, is: Doesn't Cuba have a right to choose its own destiny – and that includes a form of government that is appropriate to its own people – and not to be interfered with by other nations?'

'Yes, I believe so. The Comandante has established his own brand of Socialism which suits Cuba, and we are no longer a threat to anyone. Besides, there are other countries which are established Communists such as China, North Korea and Russia, which are left alone to conduct their own affairs and to trade freely with the rest of the world,' said Cardenzo.

'It's very true and interesting that you observed that. But it's getting late, so we must continue this discussion another time. It is very seldom that I have the opportunity to speak to someone I can trust about such matters. The next time my son comes home for a visit, you must come and see us,' said Bronski.

The Bronskis then took their leave. Carlos seemed content that he had taken the opportunity to air some of his thoughts and relieve the inner stress which is the natural result of not being able to release the mental strain. He would not now need to engage in this type of conversation with his co-workers for some time, if at all, and it was advisable that he did not do so too often because that could risk being misinterpreted by an 'ambitious friend'.

Carlos Bronski had been a high official in the Socialist Party and a strong supporter of the Revolution and the policies which the Comandante had introduced. In the early days of the Revolution, the Russians were Cuba's economic life-line and had great influence in Cuba. Wanting to show their solidarity, many Cubans adopted Russian names.

In fact, Carlos had been so influenced by the Communists that he changed – or, more precisely, made an addition to – his name. It was not known why he chose the name 'Bronski', but Carlos announced that he had changed his name, and that he was henceforth to be known and officially referred to as 'Carlos Alvarez Bronski'. His wife, Caterina, also added the name Bronski, and when their son was born, he was given the name Augusto Alvarez Bronski.

Augusto was currently attending the University of Havana and expecting to qualify as a medical doctor within five years. His father considered this a success story for the family, because it was as a result of his contacts and affiliation in the Socialist Party that Augusto had secured a place in the Medical School. It seemed that one still had to pull strings, even in a Socialist system.

Subsequently, however, Carlos Bronski had fallen out of favour with certain Party officials and was reallocated to work as a supervisor on agricultural projects in the Valle de los Ingenios. For the past few years, he had been hoping that he would be restored to favour in the Party but, so far, he had not had the call. No one, except his superiors, knew the reasons for his relegation, but he still remained a patriotic citizen, loyal to the Socialist cause, and did not complain, assuring himself that his Augusto would amount to someone important in the history of Cuba.

Cardenzo Martinez was not so politically minded as Carlos Bronski. He was more compliant than most of his countrymen. He accepted and silently supported the Revolution because he believed that it would eventually benefit his people and his country, and that those who were in control should get on with the job of carrying out their Socialist policies. He knew that Machado and Batista had not been the right people to govern Cuba, but he secretly thought that Fidel's Revolution was taking too long for the people to benefit – fifty years is a long time.

Although Cardenzo was put to work on the farms in the Valle, he had been much happier when working with his father on their little farm because he found that working for the Revolution was too regimented. When the family was first reallocated to the Valle, he felt like a man who was sentenced to an open prison. Cutting cane and setting the 'green lakes' on fire at harvest time did not give him the same satisfaction as sowing and reaping the variety of crops which he had been accustomed to nurturing from birth. He felt that there was no craft in cutting cane, and that the agricultural knowledge which he had learnt since he was a boy was being wasted. He hated it, but realised as time went on that he had to endure it for the sake of his Amelia, their two children and his ageing mother who now lived nearby, just down the Lane.

Cardenzo believed that to live in the shadow of the Iznaga Tower was not a pleasant place to be. He knew its history and it reminded him of too much unpleasantness. He shielded his daughters from the sordid history of the Valle in order not to contaminate their young minds about the cruelties of the world. He thought there would be sufficient time for them to learn about that when they grew up, and hoped that, by then, their minds would have been moulded to have tolerance, to love mankind and to appreciate the beauty of the world. In a sense, there was a conspiracy between Amelia and Cardenzo to protect their children from the harshness of the Valle, and of life, whenever possible.

But Cardenzo had to conform, and was encouraged to do so after having met many of the neighbours who were born in the Valle and who could trace their ancestry far back to the days of slavery. The brilliance of the day can make one forget that dark history, but when the sun fades into night the Valle becomes less accommodating.

The night seemed to be the commencement of the earth as the gentle breeze moved through the Valle. The sweet call of birds could be faintly heard in the distance – a peaceful and welcome interruption to the quiet of the night.

31

'Papa, what is 'assassination'? I heard Señor Bronski mention it last night,' said Candelaria. It was a word that had been on her mind all night. Her father was taken by surprise. He thought about his answer for a few moments.

'It is the removal of a king from his throne by force,' said Cardenzo.

'Which king is he, Papa?' asked Candelaria.

'Our Fidel Castro, who is like a king to us,' said Cardenzo.

'But why would they want to remove him from his throne?' asked Candelaria.

'Because some people do not know who is a good king and who is not. Some people make mistakes because they do not know what the king is about. So they want to replace him with a new king,' said Cardenzo.

Etna knew the meaning of the word 'assassination' because she had heard that word at school before. But Etna had her own questions to ask her father. She had overheard most of the conversation between her parents and Señor Bronski, but did not fully understand certain things.

'Am I not free, Papa?' asked Etna.

'What do you mean, Etna?' asked Cardenzo.

'Am I free as a bird, Papa?' asked Etna.

'Yes, you are, my Etna. And if you had wings you would be able to fly anywhere you like. Aren't you free to enjoy your life every day – to play with the animals and birds, and to see the bees make their honey? At your age, you are freer than most people and freer than your Mama and Papa. You have the whole Valle to play in. Both you and your sister are like two princesses – you are free to enjoy life and to be happy,' said Cardenzo.

'Aren't you free too, Papa?' asked Etna.

'Yes, my dear. I am free and so is your Mama. We may not be as free as a bird, but we are free to work, to eat what little we have, to see our friends, and to be with our darling daughters and enjoy our time with them here in the Valle,' said Cardenzo.

'Were you and Mama married here, Papa?' asked Etna.

'Yes, my dear. Your Mama and I were married right here. I wish we could have been married on our little farm in Camaguey, because that's where I was very happy and I think that is where I would like to be,' said Cardenzo.

'Then why don't we live there, Papa?' asked Etna.

'When our work is finished here, we will return there to live. But first, we have a duty to the Revolution and to our country to work for a better future – for a better life for you and your sister. In the meantime, we could visit Camaguey whenever we can – and that is as soon as you have a break from school,' said Cardenzo.

'But Papa, the grass does not grow in our back garden. Can't we go sooner?' asked Etna.

'Yes, I know, Etna. The grass is greener in our farm in Camaguey. But the grass is also greener down the Lane and in the fields and between the trees,' said Cardenzo.

'We love it there, Papa,' said Candelaria.

'And so you should, because there is where most of your 'friends' are. Love and enjoy the things you have, girls, because that is the way to happiness. The birds and animals come here to visit you, and if you think that you should be elsewhere, they would be confused and would not know where to go,' said Cardenzo.

'But Papa, wouldn't the birds and animals also come to visit us in Camaguey?' asked Etna.

'There are many birds there because they know that they cannot be in two places at the same time and so they have made up their minds to be happy in the place where they live,' said Cardenzo.

It was good practice to answer Etna's and Candelaria's questions. In the present climate of the Revolution, even a half-truth was better than a total untruth. Cardenzo had to be careful in giving explanations to his daughters' inquisitiveness. He was aware that children speak their minds spontaneously and innocently, and that conversations made in private about what their parents have discussed could easily be made public through the innocent mouths of their daughters. The girls were not old enough to know the difference, nor were they old enough to be discreet or diplomatic. Their parents believed that when they came of age and could make an intelligent appraisal for themselves, then there would be no need for half-truths or falsehoods.

CHAPTER THREE

UNCLE SILVIO VISITS

'Papa, Tiny is not eating her food. Could you help her?' asked Candelaria.

'Who is Tiny?' asked Cardenzo.

'One of the chicks. 'Tiny' is her new name', said Candelaria.

'Yes, I thought that chick was too skinny. The other chicks are not letting her eat,' said Cardenzo.

'It's Hungry's fault. She is eating up all the food,' said Candelaria.

'Hungry is it?' said Cardenzo. 'I will have to separate Tiny from the others, especially Hungry, so that Tiny can have her own food and not be disturbed by the others'.

'Thank you, Papa', said Candelaria.

'Your Uncle Silvio is coming to visit us today. You girls go and tell your Grandma,' said Amelia.

'Yes, Mama,' said the girls.

The girls set off down the Lane to convey the message. They were expecting to speak to the birds along the way, but these were strangely absent. It was Saturday, and there were lots of tourists visiting the Manaca Estate. That may have been the reason why the birds had taken flight. Even their school friends were not playing outside. But Etna and Candelaria were not too disappointed, as they would normally have been, because they were anxious to inform their grandmother that their uncle was visiting them that day.

When they reached their grandmother's house, they found her getting ready to go out and she was humming a tune while she did so. Mabelina was dressed in her best clothes and a grey-veiled hat, with a smart pair of shoes and a stylish 1950s handbag. Her outfit was sparkling and she looked as though she was going shopping in the fashionable stores of Havana of her youth. Her outfit was at least

34

forty years old, but it still maintained its newness as those things were seldom worn by Mabelina. She was a sight to behold. One would say that she did not wear her clothes but that her clothes wore her – she was the human equivalent of a scarecrow dressed to drive away the birds.

'Why are you dressed up, Grandma?' asked Etna.

'Because I'm going to visit a friend.'

'Why are you going to visit your friend?' asked Candelaria.

'Because she is ill and she is my good friend.'

'Mama wants you to come to lunch at twelve o'clock because Uncle Silvio is visiting us today,' said Etna.

'That good-for-nothing son is visiting today, is he?' said Mabelina.

'What is a 'good-for-nothing son', Grandma?' asked Candelaria.

'A son who has no loyalty and wastes his life away.'

'Does that mean that he is also a 'good-for-nothing uncle'?' asked Etna.

'I suppose so, dear. A son who deliberately keeps away from his family and does not even write to them for several months must be good-for-nothing,' said Mabelina.

'Does that mean that he does not love us, Grandma?' asked Candelaria.

'I am sure that he loves us, dear, but he does not show it. He misses his Papa very much and does not like to show his tears.'

'But we love him very much, Grandma,' said Candelaria.

'I am sure you do, my dears. You must tell him so when he comes,' said Mabelina. 'Tell your Mama that I will be there.'

'Can we come with you?' asked Etna.

'My friend Lourdes is very old. Do you want to see such a sick old lady?' asked Mabelina.

'But we know her from the time we were born, Grandma. She would be happy to see us too,' said Etna.

'I know. OK, you can come, so long as you are quiet. You do not want to disturb an old lady from her time of rest, do you?' said Mabelina.

'We will be quiet as a worm in the ground, Grandma,' said Candelaria.

'That will do. Remember, you promise now,' said Mabelina.

'Yes, we promise,' said Etna.

Etna and Candelaria waited for her outside, and, as Mabelina came out, she looked like a ship being launched. Her audience was just the two girls, and the birds would regret their absence to have missed such a sight. Mabelina created her own ceremony, for one could imagine the sound of whistles and the blowing of horns as she walked down the Lane with her two grand-daughters. She was just going across the rail-track to visit an old friend whom she would normally see as a matter of course every day because they were good neighbours and were helpful to one another.

But today she was stepping out in fashion, and she did not care whether her clothes were out of date or that the other neighbours were not there in numbers to observe her walk down the Lane wearing high-heeled shoes in the most awkward manner imaginable, and knowing that she did not have a peso in her expensive handbag. She played the part of a fashionable lady who had come to town to visit an old friend. Mabelina knew that she looked ridiculous as a badly dressed peacock, in shoes which were not accustomed to her distorted feet, and out of place in this semi-jungle.

Mabelina's friend was Lourdes Juliana de Santiago. She was one of the few black women who could claim to be a pure descendant of African slaves. This was due to the fact that the blood of Cuba has been greatly mixed – before and, more so, after the Revolution. Lourdes had never married, nor did she have children. She did not seem to have any relatives. No one visited her and, during the years that she lived in the shadow of the Iznaga Tower, she appeared to be a lonely woman, except for the friendship of Mabelina.

Lourdes was a private person and a mystery to the residents of the Valle. When Mabelina said that she had a friend whom she liked, she meant it, for Mabelina was the only one in whom Lourdes confided the secrets of her life.

She was born Lourdes Juliana Mocambo in Santiago de Cuba. Her parents had lived there for many years, and they often told her that when her great-grandparents first came to Cuba, they lived and worked on an estate in the small town of Palma Soriano, just north of Santiago. Lourdes grew up in Santiago without any formal education, but she loved to sing and dance from an early age. She sang and danced in the streets of Santiago and in the *Casas de la Trova* [traditional music clubs] around the town.

In her early twenties, when she was performing in one of the *Casas*, Lourdes was spotted by an impresario from the famous Havana night-club, the *Tropicana*. While her singing and dancing captivated her audiences, most of the men came to see the agility of her buttocks – one of the most fascinating aspects of her performance.

Her fame spread throughout the island. She became a celebrity, and on many occasions she was fêted by Fulgencio Batista at his private functions. She was even photographed with him in his convertible, driving along the Malecon and smiling, as a great white wave lashed the sea-wall and sprayed the passers-by. She had become known as Lourdes Juliana de Santiago – the 'Talk of Havana'.

By 1958, Lourdes was at the top of her profession and one of the most popular entertainers in Cuba. But then, on 1st January 1959, Castro defeated Batista and everything changed in the lives of the people of Cuba. Those who supported Batista and the old regime lost their positions and their property. Those who had fraternised with the old regime were considered to have supported Batista, and they also lost their possessions and their status in the new Cuban society.

The new 'King' must purge his country and establish his own regime. Many neutrals suffered because there was doubt about their neutrality or support and, since they had no way of proving it, they were also denounced. The Revolution took the view that it was better to be safe than sorry and imposed a New Order of Socialism upon the people, which further controlled them by direct means and changed the course of their history.

Lourdes Juliana de Santiago was one of those caught up in the Socialist purge. She was considered to be a supporter of Batista and, because of her public appearances with him, she had conveyed the impression that Batista was favoured by her. Since the people applauded Lourdes for her artistic ability and fame, it was suggested that some of that popularity rubbed off on Batista and make him more acceptable to the people.

Of course, Lourdes was completely innocent of the political implications of having associated with Batista and all that was contrary to the principles of the Revolution. She was unjustly accused. She was a descendant of slaves, and for such a person to have become famous and loved by the people in her own right was unheard of previously. She was merely doing what was natural to her – making use of her innate talents in order to improve herself and to make a better life for her and her family.

Lourdes was classified as an undesirable person of the Revolution and, as a result of the *Tropicana* being closed down, she found herself out of work. The *Casas de la Trova* would not employ her because they did not want to be associated with a person who was 'negatively classified' by the new regime. She became unemployable in her profession and, in due course, was sent to work – first in the tobacco farms in Pinar del Rio and then to such places as Sancti Spiritus and Matanzas after taking part in the Literacy Programme. She ended up in the Valle de los Ingenios as her final place of forced labour. That had been in 1988, twenty years ago.

'*Hola*, Mabelina. I see you brought your grandchildren with you,' said Lourdes. She was in bed when she heard Mabelina's knock on her door.

'Yes, they wanted to come to see you when they heard that you were ill,' said Mabelina.

'How are Etna and Candelaria today?' asked Lourdes.

'We are quite well,' said Etna. 'Are you ill?'

'I am not too good today, my child, but I will recover soon.'

'Is your bed a hard bed or a soft bed?' asked Candelaria.

'My bed is very hard. All beds seem very hard for me these days, which makes it difficult for me to sleep,' said Lourdes.

'Can we bring you one of our soft pillows?' asked Candelaria.

'No, my dear. I am coping all right. It is not really the bed that is hard; it is my bones that are causing me pain.'

'Couldn't you take out some of those bones so that you would not be in pain?' asked Candelaria.

'That's a good idea, Candelaria. Why didn't I think of that before? But you see I still need those bones to get me about a bit, otherwise I would not be able to get up from this bed. Too much about me now. How are both of you getting along at school? Are you studying hard?'

'Yes, and what we learn we teach the birds and animals because they cannot read or write,' said Etna.

'That's a very good idea,' said Lourdes. 'Let me speak to your Grandma now.'

'Will we see you tomorrow then?' asked Candelaria.

'I believe so, God willing,' said Lourdes.

The girls were then asked to take a seat on the big rocking-chair that was by the window. They gladly did so, as they saw the opportunity to look out of the window and observe the birds which had now returned to the Valle, and to speak between themselves about all the sounds and movements in the undergrowth that they could see or imagine.

Lourdes' home was also one of the former slave huts – scant of furniture or any hint of modern household conveniences. She was therefore no different from most of the other local residents. The bare essentials of a primitive age were provided for her survival – a chair, a small table, a bed, a narrow wardrobe, a chest of drawers, a portable gas stove and access to a water tap on the outside. The tap was a recent facility, constructed after the Revolution. When the slaves lived there, they would have obtained their water from a well or brought it in and stored it in a tank near the hut to be refilled when empty.

'How are you, my heart?' asked Mabelina.

'I am trying to fight my illness, but the temperature has me bed-ridden,' said Lourdes.

'Do you think that you should see a doctor?'

'I have never had cause to see a doctor in my life, and I don't have need for a doctor now. I only have a chill and my aching bones. I shall get over it.'

Before Mabelina could comment on her illness, Lourdes continued: 'I see that you are dressed up today. Going to a party?'

'Don't you recognise it?' asked Mabelina.

'No, I don't seem to recognise …'

'You gave me this outfit some time ago,' said Mabelina.

Lourdes raised her head from her pillow and looked more closely at Mabelina, from head to toe.

'Yes, I remember having an outfit like that. I am glad I gave it to you. You are the only person who has been a good friend to me over the years. I have no other friends now, and I lost touch with my family a long time ago. I have a few more outfits in the wardrobe. They took away almost everything from me, including all my beautiful costumes. I want you to have some more dresses before you leave.'

'But Lourdes, I have no use for any more fancy clothes. I do not go anywhere, except to see you and the other neighbours. Remember I am also an old lady. I only put on these clothes today to cheer you up. I thought that they would bring back nice memories for you.'

'Those memories are long gone, but you are right – I could not forget them. Look in that bottom drawer and you will find a green head-dress. Pass it to me,' said Lourdes.

Mabelina looked in the wooden chest of drawers and passed her the 1920s-style head-dress. Lourdes placed it on her head and gesticulated in a theatrical manner, smiling as she did so.

'Pass that mirror to me,' she said.

Mabelina handed her the mirror.

'You see how pretty it looks. I wore this one at the *Tropicana* and kept it all these years, for it was one of my favourite pieces,' said Lourdes, becoming emotional as she spoke and remembered the good times.

'You were young and happy then,' said Mabelina.

'I was treated very badly just because I had met the people who were important in Cuba at the time. I knew nothing about politics and never spoke out in favour of anyone, but they treated me as an enemy of the Revolution and made me a slave again. So here I am, in one of the slave farms and living in a slave hut at the end of my life,' said Lourdes, sadly.

'Yes, we have all suffered, but you most of all,' said Mabelina.

'My parents disowned me after the Revolutionary Committee condemned me, because they were afraid that they too would be accused for my actions. People say that the Revolution was a good thing for the country and the people, but, for me, it was a bad thing that ruined my life,' said Lourdes.

It was certainly not Mabelina's intention to bring back bad memories. She thought that, by dressing up in the clothes that Lourdes had given her, it would remind her of better times and provide some relief from the consciousness of her illness. But unfortunately, her good intentions had the opposite effect.

Mabelina could not be blamed for Lourdes' state of mind at this particular time of her visit. If she had visited another time, in the same outfit, Lourdes might not have become so emotional because her thoughts did not always dwell on her fall from favour. Too many years had passed and, in the meantime, there had been the loss of her family and general hard times with which to come to terms and to survive. She would have thought that tomorrow was yet another day in the Valle and that, although times were hard and she was in pain, they could not take away the success which she had enjoyed in her life. She was once the 'Queen of Cuba'.

'Even that handbag and shoes were special. The handbag was given to me by an American sea-captain after he had seen me perform a few times, and the shoes were also a gift, from a handsome young admirer who said that he was the son of Rockefeller, the rich American tycoon. I am glad that you could put them to good use. There is no style here in the Valle. You must have caused excitement when the neighbours saw you.'

'No one saw me, and if they did I would not have minded. I am sure that they have not seen such expensive clothes in their lives.'

'And that is the point of it. They are also trapped in this hole of a place and will never know or taste a little luxury,' said Lourdes.

'Maybe it is better that they do not. They are happy as they are because they do not know any better. When I came here it was hard for me at the beginning, but I had to put the good times behind me and learn to live a different life,' said Mabelina.

'Yes, I have heard comments about you. They say that you are the salt of the earth and the mother of everyone in the Valle.'

'I like that, since I hope they mean that I am kind and generous and not envious of others, and I am always willing to help my neighbours. I suppose I have my late husband to thank for that. He taught his family never to expect too much and, when our little farm in Camaguey was doing very well and could have made more money, he said that we should work hard but take days off to rest so that we could enjoy what we have made and earned, otherwise there would be no meaning to life.'

'Your husband was a wise man, Mabelina and now you are still here to enjoy your grandchildren and see them grow up. One cannot put a price on that. And that is what I have missed so badly – not having my family with me.'

'But you have pleasant memories of your life to fall back on.'

'It is not the same. When we were young, we did not realise how important things were that would affect us in our later life. Oh, what wouldn't I do now to have my parents with me, and to tell them that I regret to have caused them so many problems and ask their forgiveness?' said Lourdes, as her eyes began to close.

Mabelina observed that Lourdes was getting tired. She called the girls who had gone outside to play, to come and say good-bye to her. When they came in, Lourdes had already fallen asleep. So they all left the hut very quietly.

They had stayed with Lourdes for much longer than intended. Mabelina had become so absorbed in their conversation that it would have been impolite to leave sooner, and in the meantime the girls had found a new interest in a nest of ants nearby.

When they arrived back at the Martinez hut, Uncle Silvio was already there. They all embraced and kissed him.

'Hey, Mama, you look like a jewel of the 50s! Where did you get that outfit from?' exclaimed Silvio.

'None of your business! You come to visit us every six months and if we do not write to you, we do not hear from you. Why don't you get married and settle down?'

'I haven't found the right girl yet.'

'You must be looking for a rich girl then. There are none left,' said Mabelina.

'That's true. There are no rich Cuban girls left – but there are a lot of pretty foreign girls,' said Silvio.

'Those are the type of girls in whom you are interested? Girls who cannot speak Spanish and do not even know what a coconut looks like?'

'Those are the best girls, Mama. The less they know, the better for me. Who wants to be pestered every day of their life? And besides, Cuban girls are just as poor as me and all they could give me is cheeky talk.'

'Money, always money. Is that all you want from a wife?' asked Mabelina.

'But, Mama, you don't know those Havana girls. They shake their bottoms in front of you and expect you to give them the world. And if you make a mistake and marry them, before you know it, they have five children and spend the rest of their lives at home. Is that what you want for your son?'

'Why do you make up these stories? You know they are not true,' said Mabelina.

'Well that's how they seem to a young man,' said Silvio.

'You consider yourself a young man? When did you last look in the mirror? Don't you see the years are catching up with you?'

'I know all you want is more grandchildren. You have two already. Why do you want more? People must be mad to have children in these hard times when they cannot afford it,' said Silvio.

'Are you going to live the rest of your life alone then?'

'If God wills it.'

'And are you speaking to God these days?' asked Mabelina.

'I know you think I am reckless, Mama. Papa also thought the same of me. I know that there are certain things in life one must do and respect and....'

Silvio could not continue because he was about to get emotional and he was afraid that he would reveal his inner feelings for his mother and her present predicament. Thoughts of the good times on their little farm in Camaguey flooded back to his mind, and this added to the pain he felt. He was conscious of the fact that he had deserted his family by going to Havana, leaving the burden and responsibility of caring for their parents to his brother, Cardenzo. He thought himself a failure as a son, but his family did not know how much of a failure he really was.

43

Mabelina did a good impression of an aggrieved mother scolding her son, but she was really happy to see Silvio and to see that he was looking fine and seemed happy, although he was not married and did not have a steady girl-friend, so far as she knew.

'Look what I brought you, Mama – a set of enamelled cooking pots. The last time I visited you, I saw how old your pots and pans were.'

Silvio did not tell his mother that he had bought the pots at the last minute, at a bargain price, from a friend who had been granted permission to emigrate to America. The set looked new, and it would appear that the previous owner had not done much cooking since he had bought them, and that Silvio had them polished in a small shop specialising in sharpening knives and scissors.

'Before I look at your pots and pans, let me see your hands,' said Mabelina.

Silvio showed his hands.

'Just as I thought – turning black. You have been working too long at that tobacco factory. Why did you ask to go there to work when you could have been making a good living on another farm?' asked Mabelina.

It was a rhetorical question to which she already knew the answer, having discussed Silvio's work with him on numerous occasions. Mabelina also knew that, since the Revolution, he could not make a better living anywhere. The question was meant to affect his sense of loyalty for having left his family and gone to live in Havana. Mama knew best and she was aware that one of the saddest things in life was when a son leaves home and would not be seen again as often as she would like.

'I'm doing fine, Mama. I cannot tell you how much better it is to work in the tobacco factory.'

Silvio certainly could not tell his mother the reasons why he found it better. It was a field of work where the objects of production were still greatly in demand all over the world. Havana cigars carried a high reputation and value so long as they were expertly crafted and stamped with the brand name of the Havana factory.

Silvio was a skilled craftsman. He soon realised that if he could make valuable cigars for his employers, he could also, at the same time, make two a week for himself and sell them on the black market. This was a dangerous business because, if he was discovered, he could be sent to prison. He therefore had to be careful, and he learned to be very careful by learning the lessons of those who had engaged in the same enterprise, but had been careless and been caught. Silvio learned not to be greedy and, by secreting a single leaf of tobacco at a time, he was able to achieve his intended purpose quite successfully.

He did not mention his illicit activities even to his own brother, Cardenzo. To tell him would have been to involve him in his crime and thereby place that family at risk of being accused of complicity, thus adding another item to his list of failures. He also could not be seen to be too generous with his gifts because enquiring eyes would get suspicious about acquisitions which they could not afford from their official incomes alone.

It was sad that his family could not benefit from his 'enterprise'. Therefore, they remained on the borderline of survival – not that Mabelina would have accepted his generosity, including those pots and pans, if she had the slightest inkling how he had afforded them. She would have been worried to death knowing that her son was continuously in danger of being sent to prison and soiling the family's good name.

'Did you hear that '*Negroso*' has won the nomination as the Democratic Candidate for the US Presidency?' asked Silvio. He was applying this term – used as a form of endearment in Cuba – to Barack Obama.

'No, we have not heard that. We are not told anything in these parts,' said Cardenzo.

'They say that there is a possibility that he may be the first black person to be elected as President of the United States.'

'I don't believe it. No black person could become President of the United States. I can't see that happening in our lifetime,' said Cardenzo.

'But he is not completely black. He is mulatto. His mother is white and his father is black African.'

'Do you think that makes any difference? He is still a black man in the eyes of the world, and especially to people in America,' said Cardenzo.

'Everyone in Havana is talking about it. They say that his opponent, McCain, is too old and that Obama has more charisma and is a good speaker.'

'What does the Comandante say about it?' asked Cardenzo.

'Well, *'Granma'* [the official Cuban newspaper] previously said that Fidel was against Obama because his policy was to maintain the embargo on Cuba. Recently though, Fidel may be changing his mind since he heard that Obama, if he becomes President, would like to ease some of the restrictions imposed on U.S. citizens and Cubans. He has also said that Cuban citizens living in Florida would be allowed more freedom to visit their relatives and to ease the flow of money between them.'

'I thought that the Comandante was totally opposed to the US capitalist system,' said Cardenzo.

'Maybe the Comandante really believes that Obama would be more reasonable than the Presidents before. A black President may see things differently,' said Silvio. 'But remember that Fidel is no longer fully in control. It is now his brother, Raul, who is taking over, and he may make certain changes in Cuba which the US President may consider to be encouraging for him to do likewise.'

The two brothers continued to speak at length about Cuba until they were summoned by Amelia to the table for the meal that was being prepared while they talked. Conversations concerning Cuba are of an absorbing kind: emotional, heart-rending, and even at times detrimental to the participants – the truth of which is still to be told. But in the present climate, political opinions must remain in their minds, although occasionally expressed through unintentional spontaneous outbursts.

The Martinez family sat down to their meal – a simple one, as usual – and engaged in small talk about the two girls; what good girls they were; how Mabelina looked aristocratic in her 1950s outfit, and the never-changing landscape of the Valle de los Ingenios.

They spoke about the old times too, and how Mabelina and their father were so active on their little farm in Camaguey. There, both sons were still with their parents and their futures had been mapped out for them. When their father died, some years after the Revolution, their lives changed for the worse. Mabelina lost heart, but did not complain while, at first, she continued living in that memory. However, she soon realised that nothing remains the same. She was conscious of the fact that she would eventually be joining her husband, and no Revolution, even if it was destined by Heaven, could prevent that reunion.

Mabelina accepted her son's cooking pots and thanked him for his gift, but she knew that they would be packed away in some old box only to be found after her death. In that event, those pots would be the only new acquisition that would be found in her hut and, since the residents in the Valle engaged in their own rules of inheritance, the pots and pans would end up in some neighbour's kitchen as the only salvage of value in return for being the first on the scene at the moment of her passing.

The family stayed up late, talking until sleep demanded that body and mind be put to rest. Mabelina walked home, escorted by both her sons, while the two girls were put to bed. How strange it must have seemed to Cardenzo and Silvio, having to walk their mother down the dark Lane to an old shack, and eventually having to say goodnight to her and to leave her all alone with only the night owl or an unsettled bird of prey for company.

Cardenzo would be seeing her again the next day, and expected to do so for many days and years to come, but Silvio would only be seeing her the next day and not again for many weeks, if his infrequent appearances in the Valle were anything to go by. As they walked silently back up the Lane, Silvio could not have failed to feel the impact of their separation. The night hides many sins and emotions, and this was one occasion when he welcomed the darkness in the Valle for it hid the minute drops of tears which he did not want his brother to see.

That night, Silvio slept on the deteriorating family couch in the living room, where he always slept on his infrequent visits. The aroma of the evening meal lingered in the air and kept him awake for most of the night, thinking. He thought of his mother's condition and of his brother's family circumstances, and this brought more tears to his eyes.

He was lucky to have escaped their hardships and was one of the exceptional few citizens of Cuba who were enjoying a comparatively easy life. The freedom of his bachelorhood and additional income from his illicit activities gave him that advantage. But Silvio was not really better off than any ordinary citizen living in Havana. He did not own a house or an apartment and had no prospects for promotion in his employment. Even if he did, his income would not be compensatory. His pain was the greater because, although he was making extra money, he still could not help his family.

When one goes to bed and cannot sleep, the mind wanders and all the problems of the world appear. Solutions and more problems are seen, but the invoker can do nothing about them until the light of day. However, by then, it is all forgotten.

Silvio tried hard to dismiss his family's problems from his mind and was able to do so a little when he realised that he was once again actually sleeping in the Valle de los Ingenios. The stillness and quietness of the night affected him. He imagined that he was locked away in the complete darkness of an ancient tomb, never to see light again. There seemed to be an absence of external life. The birds and wild animals, the small creatures of the Valle were all asleep, and not even night predators reminded him that there was life outside that room.

Silvio found the silence maddening. The Valle was such a contrast to where he lived in Central Havana, where a human cry, or the screams of a mad-man, or the slamming of the doors of an old Chevrolet automobile amid the roar of the traffic along the Malecon could be heard at any time of the night. And if there was ever a quieter night, he could always rely on the barking of a stray mongrel dog disappointed that it was not able to find scraps of food.

Even if that dog was successful in his endeavours that night, or any night, Silvio could rely on the constant lashing of the rocks by the angry waves along the Malecon, which reminded him that there was always some activity on the outside and that he was not alone, should he forget the warning of the Fort cannon every night at nine o'clock – a solemn moment, an echo from the past – reminding

Habaneros that they must not sleep too soundly because there were pirates in the waters, and, in modern times, that they should beware because there might be another 'Bay of Pigs' on the horizon.

Silvio did his duty by visiting his family. He found no beauty in the environment in which they lived – the scavenging of tourist dollars in that disreputable place did not appeal to him. It was not the same as the sense of belonging which he had felt on the family's farm in Camaguey.

He thought the Valle unfriendly, seemingly poised to protest at any moment and ready to be suppressed. He was an adult and no longer had the mind set of adolescence. It seemed that Havana had robbed him of his innocence and made him indifferent to the beauty of nature and the countryside.

At breakfast the next morning, the two brothers continued their conversation. Cardenzo had slept well but Silvio had a restless night and was irritable, which he put down to his lack of sleep. But even if he had slept soundly for twenty-four hours, he still would have been grumpy. Silvio hated the Valle, but in truth he also hated Havana and, psychologically, he had to generate a certain mental attitude to return there. This mental attitude was reflected in his conversation that morning.

'I sincerely believe that Cuba will return to capitalism in the not too distant future,' said Silvio.

'How did you come to that conclusion when our Revolution has been successful and a new society of Socialism has resulted?' asked Cardenzo.

'Cuba hasn't a chance in hell of successfully maintaining the Socialist system. There are too many negative forces stacked against it. I say this because the world is not real. Cuba has been suffering the hardships and consequences of an embargo imposed by the US, and the rest of the world participates in their unlawful enterprise without criticism or justice. How could the UN, comprising the intelligentsia of the world, condone such unlawful treatment? Just think about it. The world is no better today than it was two hundred years ago, when the power of the gun-boat and the cannon dictated the principles of right and wrong. This is our predicament. Cuba would like to go its own way but is not permitted to do so by the swirling force of the cowboy's rope determined to subdue it.'

'All this is only temporary, Silvio. The world must come to its senses and realise that injustice is taking place. Those ropes you mentioned will eventually be cut and Cuba will be allowed to co-exist.'

'Yes, brother, the world eventually changes. But, in the meantime, Cuba has to suffer and her progress would be hampered for another fifty years. How long must we suffer before change can come?' asked Silvio.

'As long as it takes.'

'And who would be answerable for that suffering?'

'The people who have caused it,' said Cardenzo.

'We know who is responsible. Are you saying that the US would ultimately be responsible?'

'If they are responsible, yes.'

'Therefore we could expect the US to be in the 'Dock of Justice' to answer for its crimes – not only those committed in Cuba but in other parts of the world?' asked Silvio.

'Yes, just like other leaders, such as Slobodan Milosevic and Radovan Karadzic of Serbia and Saddam Hussein. All will eventually be judged and punished.'

'I think, my brother, that you are making a mistake. The US believes that she is doing no wrong. She believes that her actions are proper and that everyone else is in the wrong. It is an attitude of mind which the US adopts in order to justify her illegalities. So far as one can see, she would escape justice because she is the mightiest military force and there is no other to enforce judgement,' said Silvio.

'So you are saying that the US can do anything and still escape being held accountable? That there could be more 'Bay of Pigs' incidents until our island is unlawfully conquered, and the rest of the world would just stand by and let it happen?' asked Cardenzo.

'But Cardenzo, my brother, didn't George Bush Jnr. say that his actions were directed by God? He said that he is a Christian and therefore believes that he is doing what is right. The American people believe him and support him because they do not want to deny their faith. Therefore, I am convinced that Cuba would revert to capitalism and be controlled again by the US. "As in the beginning, so shall it be in the end". Jesus suffered and died for a cause which any sane person would accept was right. His cause and mission was far greater than Cuba's; therefore how could you deny that the just and innocent would not also be overcome?'

'The people of Cuba would not allow it.'

'Brother, it is not what the people want or what is good for them, but what the prevailing circumstances are at the time. The World Order is stacked against them and they would be forced to bend,' said Silvio.

'But how can this come about when there have now been five decades of Socialism in Cuba?'

'Well, this change could take place in two ways. The first is by force of arms. The second is by a silent revolution,' said Silvio.

'What do you mean by a "silent revolution"?'

'By that I mean that the external pressures placed upon Cuba would be so great that it would be forced to change its policies and to revert to capitalism. This process would be achieved quietly, without ceremony – small changes from time to time, making inroads and departures from the ideologies of Socialism so that the people would not observe the changes until it is too late and, by then, they would have accepted it. You must not forget the fact that all is not perfect in Cuba. I would also add that the young people of Cuba, born years after the Revolution, will eventually demand change,' said Silvio.

'So you think that the Revolution and Socialism were wrong to have taken place?' asked Cardenzo.

'No, I am not saying that. Revolution and Socialism were right for Cuba. I also believe that Socialism is the right ideology for the rest of the world – a socialism that is just and fair.'

'When do you think that this 'New Capitalism' would be achieved, and would we live better lives?' asked Cardenzo.

'No, we would not live better lives – whether it is Old or New Capitalism. Remember that I am only suggesting what could happen, not that I would want it to happen, unless it is in the form of the 'New Socialism' as I have mentioned. If Cuba returned to full capitalistic ideologies, that would result in all the inequalities and moral and pecuniary degradation recurring – for man is fifty per cent greedy, thirty per cent selfish and only twenty per cent humanitarian. There would be great discontent as the rich get richer and the poor get poorer, which would set the scene for a new Revolution in the twenty-first century and set Cuba back for another hundred years.'

'You seem to speak very knowledgably of the politics of our country, Silvio.'

'I spend my time reading a lot, to keep up with world affairs from the foreign magazines brought in by the tourists. I do not only spend my time with, you know, women, as Mama thinks. I know that she thinks that I am wasting my life, but a man must have a hobby or an interest in life, especially when most opportunities are not open to him.'

'You surprise me today. You are no longer just the carefree brother I once knew. Mama would really be surprised to know that you have retained some common sense in order to assess all that's going on around you,' said Cardenzo.

'We all have to change some time. It's the same for a country. It is the nature of man to change. Time changes man and he forgets the pains of the past, but it is only with time that the cycle is complete and he is back to where he started – lessons are not learnt.'

'Another philosophy from your various readings?'

'Maybe. I just cannot remember where I get these things from,' said Silvio. 'But Cuba must learn its lesson and not repeat the same mistakes of the past. If change is to come, then Cuba must not allow the Americans to come into the country in large numbers, for they would prostitute our women, swamp the island and demean our way of life. After fifty years of want, it would be a dangerously tantalizing prospect for the majority of our people.'

It seemed that the two brothers had been speaking for hours. Etna and Candelaria were summoned from the back garden, away from their preoccupation with the chicks. Tiny seemed to have benefited from the separation and looked more perky and happy. Gallina grinned in recognition that Hungry had one portion less and would have to survive as everyone else on their specific rations. The girls were called in and invited to accompany their uncle, who was about to visit his mother again before he left for Havana. It was five o'clock in the afternoon and Silvio, Etna and Candelaria walked down the Lane towards Mabelina's house, holding hands.

'Who is that man speaking to Mama?' asked Silvio.

'Señor Bronski,' said Etna.

'Oh yes, I remember him now. I just can't seem to like that man.'

'Why don't you like him, Uncle?' asked Candelaria.

'It's just a feeling, Candelaria. Don't worry about it,' said Silvio.

They came up to Mabelina and Señor Bronski.

'I've just come to say good-bye to you, Mama,' said Silvio.

'Leaving already?' asked Mabelina.

'Yes, you know this place drives me crazy,' said Silvio.

'So this is your other son?' asked Bronski.

'Silvio, this is Señor Bronski,' said Mabelina, introducing them.

'We have met before,' said Silvio.

'Oh yes, so we have. On that occasion I seem to remember that you were ill,' said Bronski.

'I was not ill, I was tired,' said Silvio.

'You looked too healthy and strong to be tired,' said Bronski.

'If you really want to know, I was disgusted with this place. The people live here like rats in the field,' said Silvio.

'Be careful what you say, son,' said Mabelina.

'That's good advice. You should listen to your mother,' said Bronski.

'And who are you to give me advice?'

'Señor Bronski is an official of the Socialist Party, son,' said Mabelina.

'So he is one of those who are responsible for the poor conditions here,' said Silvio.

'I used to have an influential position in the Administration,' said Bronski.

'What are you saying? Have they demoted you?' asked Silvio.

'The Regime has been good to me. I am now a Supervisor here in the Valle and my son, Augusto is studying medicine at the University of Havana. I still have some influence.'

'If you have any influence you should be living in the Mansion House, not in one of these slave huts as the rest of the people here.

53

You must have done something bad for you to be treated this way,' said Silvio.

'I have not done anything bad. I just had a misunderstanding with some of the Ministers. Nothing serious. You would not understand.'

'I understand very well. You believe that everyone who still supports the Revolution is a fool. I also understand that the people in this Valle are suffering silently, because if they speak openly about their difficulties they would be thrown into prison. Why should young children, such as my nieces here, have to suffer because our leaders do not know how to run our country?'

'You don't know what you are saying. I believe that they are doing a good job,' said Bronski.

'Do you deny that there is still a privileged class in our society – people living the high life as if there was no Revolution, while the majority of our people are suffering?'

'Where do you see this high-living?' asked Bronski.

'I can take you to many places around the island and show you proof of it,' said Silvio. 'And the Government knows about it but they prefer to pretend that it does not exist.'

'Maybe it is those people who are pretending to live the high life, as they knew it before the Revolution, but in fact, they are just as poor as the rest of us,' said Bronski.

'And, anyway, why is your name "Bronski"? Were you pretending to be a Russian aristocrat in order to gain favours when they had some influence here?' asked Silvio. 'Or do you think that you would be accepted in Russia as an equal because you changed your name to "Bronski"?'

'I am loyal to the Socialist Party and to the Revolution. I do not have to give you an explanation of why I changed my name.'

'It's like a black man pretending to be white when the majority of society is white and has all the influence. And you, a mestizo, of all people!' said Silvio.

'Mabelina, your son is certainly aggressive towards me. He must think that I am his enemy. He is different from Cardenzo, whom I consider a gentleman.'

'Señor, my son has his own mind. He says and does what he feels. Don't take him too seriously,' said Mabelina, reluctant to criticise Silvio in front of Bronski because she secretly believed that her son was speaking the truth, although she did not like the manner in which he was saying it.

'You see, Mama, if everyone keeps his place and remains silent then he would be considered a patriot of the Revolution. Right or wrong, it seems that Señor Bronski and his associates would have us suffer for the Revolution. And what do they give us in return? Bad housing, a lack of opportunity, a ration book where the necessities of life are controlled, and a country where a taxi-driver earns more than a doctor or a school-teacher.'

'Your son must really be careful. His statements can be taken as unpatriotic and he could be accused of being disloyal to our Government. He is lucky he is making this outburst to me and in this quiet place, otherwise he would be arrested. Mabelina, I have too much respect and appreciation for you and your family for me to take offence. I must now say *"Adios"* and hope that the next time we meet, Silvio, you would have gotten rid of your anger,' said Bronski.

Silvio had certainly given vent to his anger which had been boiling over during this visit to the Valle, but it appeared that he had chosen the wrong man on whom to release it. Señor Bronski, although conceited, was a good friend of the Martinez family and should not have been attacked in such a dramatic fashion. Silvio should also have considered that friendship could often conflict with patriotism and that, when Señor Bronski had time to reflect on what was said to him, he might have placed his patriotic duty first and still accused Silvio of being disloyal to the Revolution. There was always a risk of danger in speaking too openly about politics, even to a good family friend.

But Silvio was in no state of mind to listen to reason. His sleepless night had the effect of intoxication. It made him irritable and belligerent and, added to this, the guilt which he felt made a strong cocktail for disaster in human behaviour. Silvio felt guilty about the poor living conditions of his mother, and of Cardenzo and his family, and his inability to help them. By going to Havana, he felt that he had abandoned them to a place of negative possibilities. He also felt guilty for his own misdemeanours, and the possibility of disgrace upon the family name if they were to be discovered by the tobacco company. He feared that one day he would return to work and that, in one of the factory's regular announcement or reading sessions, his name would be called out and it would be made public that he was stealing from the company and was therefore unpatriotic. He secretly felt afraid and ashamed.

Although he had directed his anger towards Señor Bronski, he may, on a calmer day, have realised that his anger was not personally against his family's friend, but against the Revolution itself for having, as he saw it, failed the people and subjecting them to fifty years of hardship.

Etna and Candelaria listened attentively to the conversation and observed the mood of their Uncle Silvio. They had never seen him so aggressive before and must have been confused about the reasons why he was so angry, having known him all their lives as a loving and gentle uncle and a figure of great fun in the presence of his family. The details of that conversation would have gone down into the archives of the girls' brains, to be analysed and pondered upon in times of silent tranquillity.

CHAPTER FOUR

INVENTIVE MINDS

After Silvio took his leave, the girls' mood changed as they walked back to their house. The day's tourists had already left the Manaca Estate and the local residents would have been settling down to a quiet Sunday evening. It seemed strange that there were no birds about when there was no apparent reason for their absence. But the girls were not too unhappy about that as they were not in a talkative mood. If they had seen any birds and not spoken to them, the girls would have felt sad that they had neglected their friends.

Walking up the Lane, they observed the unusual behaviour of a swarm of ants. They were busy preparing their nest with leaves, dry twigs and anything that would give shelter to their abode. In fact, it was more than that. They were, in effect, fortifying their abode as if expecting a flood or a destructive hurricane.

When Etna and Candelaria reached closer to their home, the blue sky began to fill up with black smoke. They heard the faint voices of men shouting in the Valle. It seemed that the men were burning the sugar-cane in readiness for harvesting, or burning dry leaves to prepare the soil for planting a new crop. The black smoke lingered overhead and cast an eerie shadow over the Valle. The local birds may have sensed the oncoming of the smoke and decided to take up temporary residence elsewhere. There was not a breath of wind and the trees were motionless as if caught in the doldrums of the ocean.

As the girls entered their house, they thought they heard the Iznaga Tower bell ring twice, but they did not pay that any particular attention because they knew it was impossible, and they were anxious to go inside and get away from these unusual occurrences.

When they went to give their 'friends' their last feed for the night, the girls found them very subdued and unresponsive. Dulcina, Greedy and Hungry were normally excited at the prospect of food,

57

but they now showed no interest. So far as the girls were aware, the chicks were not ill and had been active all day until the coming of the evening. The sun was about to set and Dulcina should have been crowing his throaty chorus in the Valle, but the absence of that sound drew the girls' attention once more to the unusualness of the evening.

They told their parents that they had forgotten to thank Silvio for their presents – two pretty dresses bought in Havana. They tried them on and were both very pleased. They said that they would write to their uncle to thank him and to tell him that they loved him.

'That's a good idea, girls. Your Uncle Silvio will appreciate it. Good of you to think of that,' said Amelia.

'It was Grandma who reminded us. She said that we must tell him that we love him,' said Etna.

'And so you should. He seems to me to be very lonely and, if I may say so, a little unhappy,' said Amelia.

'You all must not worry about Uncle Silvio. He can take care of himself,' said Cardenzo.

'Uncle Silvio seemed to be very angry with Señor Bronski,' said Etna.

'Oh. What did Uncle Silvio say to him? asked Cardenzo.

'He told him many things about the Revolution which made Señor Bronski very unhappy,' said Etna.

'Grandma was also unhappy, Papa,' said Candelaria.

'I shall speak to her,' said Cardenzo.

'Papa, why is everything so different today?' asked Etna.

'What do you mean, dear? What is so different?'

'The black smoke from the burning of the sugar-cane has covered the whole Valle. It is the first time I have seen it so black,' said Etna.

'Nothing unusual about that. I have seen it darker,' said Cardenzo.

'It's the wind, my dear. When there is no wind, the smoke lingers overhead,' added Amelia.

'The ants usually play in the evening before they go to sleep. This evening, they were busy protecting their nests as if they were expecting a hurricane,' said Etna.

'Maybe they are expecting a hurricane,' said Cardenzo.

'But the hurricane season has already passed,' said Amelia.

'Etna, tell Papa about the bell,' said Candelaria.

'What bell?'' asked Cardenzo.

'The Iznaga Tower bell, Papa. Candelaria and I thought that we heard it ring twice.'

'But the Tower bell is fixed to the ground. It cannot ring any more,' said Amelia.

'The last time that bell made any sound was when it was taken down from the tower years ago,' said Cardenzo.

'And the chicks and Dulcina?' asked Candelaria.

'What about them?' asked Amelia.

'They are usually very noisy when we feed them before they go to bed. Today, they did not eat and were all very quiet,' said Candelaria.

'Again, nothing unusual about that. Maybe they were not hungry or were affected by the black smoke,' said Cardenzo.

'Papa, I am afraid. Do you think that we are going to have another hurricane?' asked Candelaria.

'Perhaps. It would not be too unusual to have one in this month of November,' said Cardenzo. 'So make sure all the doors and windows are secured.'

'It's time for you to go to bed now girls,' said Amelia.

The girls dutifully obeyed their mother, said goodnight and went to bed. They were very tired following the events of the day, the excitement of seeing their Uncle Silvio, the presents he had brought them and the unusual occurrences which they thought they had experienced that seemed strange to them.

Their parents waited for Etna and Candelaria to fall asleep before they could address their daughters' fears. Cardenzo and Amelia knew that the incidents were strange, but did not want to confirm the girls' fears so as to alarm them. Young children do not understand the workings of the mind, and therefore do not know how to react when an oddity presents itself. Some people are convinced that they have seen UFOs, but when the evidence is closely examined it is proved that they were mistaken – or were they? Cardenzo and Amelia thought that the girls were confused and mistaken and, if that was the case, they should not be concerned too much for the girls' welfare and sanity.

But this was too simplistic an answer. Everything the girls had observed that evening was quite feasible and would not have merited comment except that the intensity and consecutive nature of the incidents made them extraordinary – especially when they said that they heard the Iznaga Tower bell ring twice. Cardenzo and Amelia could easily have accepted all the other incidents as appearing unusual to the girls – they were so closely attuned to nature and the elements that they would have observed the slightest change when others could not.

The girls had played with every living creature that inhabited their surroundings and knew their various idiosyncrasies well. If the local family of ants had decided to build a fortification for safety, when they already had a secure and well defended home, the girls would have known that was unusual. The girls could speak to the birds and the animals, but those creatures could not respond in any explicit manner. Otherwise they would have been told the actual reasons for their apprehension. Was it not just the girls' sixth but 'seventh' sense that made them more cognizant of what their 'friends' wanted to convey?

But Cardenzo and Amelia did not consider a more obvious cause for their daughters' apprehension – 'superstition' and a belief in things unexplainable. In Cuba, superstition was rife in the past and, although the people are now more enlightened, it still affects and influences many. It is a custom that is very difficult to eradicate. So, for example, it was said that if a rooster crowed three times without getting an answer, that meant that some tragedy might occur. Similarly, if an owl flew over at night and one could hear the sound of its wings and its screech, that too was a sign of tragedy. If a salt-cellar fell on the floor and broke into pieces, the only way to forestall bad luck was to pick up some of the spilt salt and throw it over your left shoulder.

As in the examples of what the girls had recounted, they believed that the birds, the animals and the black smoke suggested something unusual was about to take place. However, Cardenzo and Amelia could still not account for the ringing of the Tower bell and put that down as mistaken identification of the actual sound. So superstition may have been the reason for the girls' reaction, but their parents did not consider it because they thought that the girls were too young to understand the meaning of the word 'superstition' and the influences which it possessed.

Cardenzo and Amelia thought that the girls did not know of such things. But, for example, the girls may have known that, if they did spill salt, they had to pick up some and throw it over their left shoulder in order to avoid bad luck. Most people, wherever they live, know of this superstitious act from an early age, having been told about it by their parents, grandparents or their peers. Etna and Candelaria may have used their imagination and exaggerated the 'unusual occurrences', or may have applied what they had overheard from the casual conversations of others. Cardenzo and Amelia, therefore, did not think that there was anything to be concerned about. They went to bed with the thought that the girls were merely growing up and were naturally acquiring inventive minds.

At breakfast the next morning, Etna said to her parents, 'I had a very strange dream in the night'.

'What was it, dear?' asked Amelia.

'I dreamt that Candelaria and I were speaking to some African slaves,' said Etna.

'And I had the same dream too, Mama,' said Candelaria.

'You can't have the same dream, Candelaria. Everyone's dream is different,' said Amelia.

'But we did, Mama! Etna told me her dream and it was the same,' said Candelaria.

'OK, let Etna tell us about her dream and we shall see if it is the same,' said Amelia.

'In my dream, I heard someone calling my name: "Etna, are you there? Etna, are you there?" I woke up and realised Candelaria had too, and saw five black people standing near the bed. I asked them: "Who are you? What do you want?" The older man said, "Do not be afraid, we are the Abufera family. This is Luther, my son and Rose, his wife, and their children Toto and Daisy."

I said to them: "Why have you come to see us – we are only two young girls?" and the man said: "We know, but you are the purest in the land and only to the purest do these apparitions come. Be not afraid."

I said: "We are not afraid, but we do not know you."

He said: "That's true, but you are known to us and you are listed as good friends of every living creature. Your goodness has come through the ages and we are here to seek your help."

I said: "But how can we help you? We are only children."

The old man then said: "We were slaves of Señor Angel, the Master of this Valle. We were seized and brought to this land to work on his plantations. We suffered many years of hard work and cruelty. My wife died before our grandchildren were born. We tried to live that new life imposed upon us, and accepted all the hardships and punishments because we believed that in the next life our happiness would depend on how we endured all the evils on this earth. But the punishment became too much for us and we were forced to try to escape. We fled to the hills and were on the run for three weeks before we were recaptured by Señor Angel's ravenous dogs which tore into our bodies with their sharp teeth. We were saved from near death, which would have been a welcome release from our daily life.

"Señor Angel took us back to the Valle and told the other slaves that it was useless for them to try to escape because they would always be caught and punished. That night, as we slept, Señor Angel's men came and slaughtered us and threw our bodies into the water-well near the rail-track. Our bodies were covered up with dirt. The manner of our death and swift disposal has created a vacuum of eternal unrest for our souls, unless our remains can be found and our traditional ceremony of burial be performed. This is your task and the reason for our appearance: to find the water-well, search for our remains and, when found, to perform the ritual of our burial. Only then would we rest in peace in the land of our fathers."

Etna spoke very clearly and in detail of the conversation with the African slaves as if they were repeating the conversation a second time to a new audience. She used language and words which were not in her normal vocabulary. She was concentrated on what she was saying as if reading a script, and appeared to be another person, determined to get across her message. Cardenzo and Amelia were shocked by how Etna, their young and innocent daughter, could relate such a strange tale, but they did not outwardly show signs of their amazement.

'Was this your dream as well, Candelaria?' asked Cardenzo.

'Yes, Papa. I met them and spoke to them too,' said Candelaria.

'What did you say to them?' asked Cardenzo.

'The young boy asked if we were also slaves. I told him "No", and Etna said that we had a Revolution and now all the people are happy.'

'Is this the truth, girls? You have not made it up to play a joke on your Mama and Papa?' asked Amelia.

'No, Mama, it is the truth. It was real to us,' said Etna.

'But you said that it was a dream,' said Amelia.

'Yes, but like a real dream,' said Candelaria.

'We would not lie to you, Mama. Our dream was real,' said Etna.

'I know, dear, but that makes it more difficult to understand,' said Amelia. 'What does your Papa think?'

'Etna and Candelaria, you are my lovely daughters. You are the cherries of our hearts. I have no doubt that you are telling your Mama and Papa the truth about what you dreamt. But I want to tell you that people have all sorts of dreams. Some are realistic, that is to say they seem very real at the time, while others are fantasies of the mind. Whatever dreams they are, they all have their own interpretation. To interpret a dream is very difficult and, therefore, most dreams are misunderstood. Both of you girls are growing up, and you will see and hear many things. What you see and hear in the day may stay in your minds and appear in your dreams at night. There is nothing unusual about this. We all have these types of dreams,' said Cardenzo.

'But, Papa, we told you that, because the family of ants were protecting their nests, a hurricane was coming. And Gallina, Dulcina and the chicks were very quiet and not eating their food. And the wild birds went away. Maybe all these things happened because they knew that strangers were coming to visit us,' said Etna.

Cardenzo and Amelia continued to be shocked. Etna had displayed an adult understanding of certain of the superstitious occurrences of the previous evening for which they had given her no credit. It all suggested that the girls' strange 'dream' had taken place and that they were telling the truth about what they had heard and seen. But superstitions are only fictitious fantasies, rejected by some, although believed by many. Cardenzo and Amelia were not on the side of the believers, and wondered how their young daughters could have a different belief to their own. They therefore rejected the occurrences of the previous evening as having no connection with the girls' dream. Nevertheless, they were of course concerned for the welfare of their daughters.

'Were you afraid when you had your dream?' asked Cardenzo.

'And was it a bad dream?' asked Amelia.

'No, Mama. It was not a bad dream, and we were not afraid,' said Etna.

Cardenzo and Amelia were then satisfied that the best course of action was for the girls not to tell anyone else about their dream – that they should certainly not speak about it at school – and that in time they would forget all about it. Cardenzo and Amelia could themselves also not speak about it to anyone, in case their daughters might be ridiculed or thought of as being mad. They believed that the girls might have been hallucinating, and that the reactions of birds and animals are different from human beings, which could account for all the 'happenings' in the Valle the previous evening.

Cardenzo and Amelia decided to keep a close eye on their girls, to observe their every movement and eavesdrop on most of their conversations in order to try and see whether they were affected by their dream or were consistent in the facts of their story. When the girls went to sleep that night, their parents sat up for most of the night to see whether any intruders were disturbing the girls' sleep or whether they were sleep walkers or spoke in their sleep.

Cardenzo and Amelia maintained their vigil as 'night watchmen' and did not retire to their own bed until around 5:00 a.m. in the belief that it would soon be daylight and no intruder would dare to appear as dawn was about to break. They did not know that most people dream between the hours of four and six o'clock, when the mind has overcome the initial stages of the day's activities, worries, problems or concerns and relaxes into a world of its own. At this point, the dreamer's mind is adrift, floating in space, and receptive to the slightest turbulence that attracts its attention. And, in space, there are many turbulences which are desperately on the look-out for a house of refuge – the stronger and more determined will prevail.

The next morning, bright and early as usual, Etna and Candelaria awoke. They did what they did every morning: feeding Gallina, Dulcina and the chicks, as well as the other birds. They spoke to all their 'friends' and wished them a pleasant day. Tiny was at last showing signs of putting on weight and was not unduly distressed by the separation. She now engaged in conversations with the other chicks. The usual chatter of all the birds and animals, in and out of the cage, had returned.

The girls knew that everything had returned to normal and nothing strange was in the air. If there was, the girls would only know of it, or lack of it, by the reactions of their 'friends'. By looking into their eyes, they would have detected an indication of their moods. But, today, Dulcina was blinking and quivering more than usual. Perhaps he was too busy concentrating on his eating, having missed yesterday's dinner; the four chicks were the same – restless, nervous, erratic and not affording the girls the opportunity to look them in the eyes.

If all else failed, Gallina, too adaptable for her own good, knew everything that was going on in the Valle. One look into her eyes would tell the girls the nature and condition of things – a change in the weather or a warning of some future unforeseen disaster. If Gallina gave such indications, she was sure to reinforce them by expressions and contortions of her face and her grinning display of teeth. One must be able to observe and read the signs, and Etna and Candelaria were able to do so. Birds and animals cannot formulate the spoken word but they are more sensitive to the silent and invisible world.

That morning, the girls greeted their parents and proceeded to have their breakfast as if nothing had happened.

'Did you sleep well?' asked Amelia.

'Yes, Mama, very well', said Etna.

'Did you also sleep well, Candelaria?' asked Amelia.

'Yes, Mama.'

'And did you have any dreams?' asked Cardenzo.

'Dreams about anything?' added Amelia.

65

Both girls replied that they did not have any dreams of any kind, and that they had slept soundly through the night. Cardenzo and Amelia looked at each other and may have thought that their decision to ignore the dream about the slaves and not to speak about it further was a wise one. As they expected, the dream – or nightmare – would eventually vanish from the girls' memory and they would be back to normal once again.

But while he was at work that day, Cardenzo knew that he was still disturbed about all the happenings of the last two days. He made up his mind to speak to Mabelina and get her opinion. So, after work, he went directly to his mother's house and told her about the girls' dream.

'Son, I have been hearing voices in the Valle for many years. I have been hearing crying, weeping and wailing and voices calling out. At first, I thought it was the wind, but when it happened again and again, I knew it was not that,' said Mabelina.

'But, Mama, you never mentioned this to me before!' said Cardenzo.

'I never mentioned it to anybody because I did not want people to think that I was going out of my head, and for them to put me in a mad house,' said Mabelina.

'So you believe that Etna and Candelaria have seen and heard spirits, and that their 'dreams' were real?' asked Cardenzo, more worried than before.

'I don't know whether they have seen anything, but they may have heard voices when they were in deep sleep and mixed them up with other dreams. From what you told me, they seem to have seen apparitions of slaves. I have not seen any of those things, but I distinctly remember a few times when I heard the sound of a railway locomotive, stopping and starting, at the back of this house. It was so real to me, but I thought that it could not be true and that I must have been dreaming, because that railway track has been disused for so many years,' said Mabelina.

'I knew that we had cause to be worried. Amelia and I stayed up last night to observe the girls while they were sleeping, but we did not see or hear anything unusual. We decided not to do anything about it, hoping that they would forget it,' said Cardenzo.

'But son, you cannot see a dream. You can see someone sleep-walking, but you cannot see them dreaming. You cannot see someone else's apparition. The only one who can see an apparition is the person to whom the apparition appears. When I heard the voices crying and wailing, I wondered why I could not see the persons who were obviously suffering. I was confused, but I have now come to accept that I will never have that opportunity,' said Mabelina.

'Do you think that my daughters have psychic powers, so that they can see and detect things which we adults cannot?' asked Cardenzo.

'I do not know, but I would not be surprised if they do. Those girls live so close to Mother Nature that they can probably anticipate certain events. When they visit me, they often tell me things which contradict my own beliefs or reason. Sometimes they visit me when the sky is black, thunder is rolling and the wind is furious – all suggesting that heavy rain is about to fall at any moment. But then they assure me: 'The rain will not fall today, Grandma. The birds are busy feeding their young. If the rain was about to fall, the birds would have waited to catch the young worms brought out by the rain.' They are usually proved right and the rain does not fall, even when it seemed obvious that it would. They say things like that,' said Mabelina.

'What can I do then?' asked Cardenzo. 'We are so worried about them.'

'You cannot do anything, but you should not worry. Apparitions do not hurt anyone – especially your innocent young daughters. They are very intelligent girls, and if they can understand the wild birds and animals, no harm would come to them,' said Mabelina.

'Amelia is so worried that she cannot sleep,' said Cardenzo.

'Since you are so worried, you should have the girls examined by a doctor and, at the weekend, take them to the seaside,' said Mabelina.

'That's a very good idea. After they are examined, I will take them and Amelia for a break by the sea. They have been so confined to the Valle that it is stifling their minds,' said Cardenzo.

CHAPTER FIVE

THE CLINIC

When Cardenzo returned home, he found both girls at the table, writing a letter to their Uncle Silvio to thank him for his gifts and to say that they were missing him and hoped that he would visit them again soon. They added a postscript: 'Grandma likes the pots and pans but she has not used them as yet.'

'And you can also tell him that we will be spending the weekend at La Boca,' said Cardenzo.

'Papa, are we really going to the beach?' asked Etna.

'Oh, yes. We will go on Saturday and return on Sunday evening. I still have to confirm it with Señor Anore, but it should be OK because he is going to Matanzas this weekend,' said Cardenzo.

The girls were elated, but Amelia was surprised when Cardenzo made the announcement. She knew right away that it was a good idea for the girls to get away from the Valle for however short a time. She was coming to believe that the girls might become affected by their dream which could make them depressed. She was happy to see that they responded in a positive and excited manner, and they were reassured that Mabelina would feed the chicks so they would not have to worry about their friends.

'We will have to tell Grandma not to forget to feed the other wild birds and animals too,' said Candelaria.

'She knows,' said Cardenzo. 'And tomorrow, Amelia, you must take the girls to the Clinic for a physical and psychiatric examination. It is good that our medical services are available to us all at no cost. The Comandante always boasts about our health care, so make sure you make use of it tomorrow,' said Cardenzo.

'I will take them immediately after breakfast, to try and get ahead of the crowd that usually forms outside,' said Amelia.

'Well, we must have breakfast earlier tomorrow,' said Cardenzo.

68

The next morning, Amelia, Etna and Candelaria found themselves waiting in a long queue at the Clinic. Amelia had wanted to get there much earlier to be near the head of the queue, but that was always going to be difficult since she had to prepare her daughters for the Clinic, and they, in turn, would not leave their home until they had fed all the birds and animals and engaged in their daily conversations. On reaching the Reception desk, they were given a numbered ticket, No. 15, to see the doctor.

Waiting in a doctor's surgery at any time is not a pleasant experience, especially if that surgery is full of children and those children are the patients. Amelia would have known this and dreaded it. Yes, the medical services are free – a tribute to the Revolution – but what the citizens do not pay in cash they pay in stress and mental frustration.

A mother cannot ask a young child to sit quietly and expect her polite request to be obeyed. Such a boy runs about, shouts, interferes with everything in sight and creates mayhem as if the request was an invitation to cause every malfeasance known to him at his age. If he is not causing a nuisance alone, he is quickly joined by his new friends in games causing havoc to everyone in the waiting room except his mother or carer who is unconcerned, being engaged in loud conversation with others. Babies cry, as they do, and mothers pacify them with a spontaneous offer of the breast. If that is not the baby's urgency, a change of its clothing transforms the waiting room into a nursery.

Chaos reigns in the waiting room of a Cuban clinic and everyone suffers without complaint. Mothers may be there to obtain a cure for their children, but the agility of the young ones suggests that they are physically fit and that they are there only to escape school and to get a break from being instructed on the Revolution and rules of discipline.

Etna and Candelaria were mere observers of the other children's activities, and they must have realised that their true friends and playmates were of the feathered kind – well-behaved, responding to affection and not complaining even though, for their own safety, they are caged up for most of their lives.

69

About two hours later, Amelia and the girls were relieved from their ordeal when they were called in to see the doctor. Amelia told him about the girls' dream, and said that she thought they should be given a medical examination. After ascertaining that the girls were not in pain, did not have a fever or complain of any ailments, the doctor was of the opinion that nothing was physically wrong with them, but recommended that they should see the psychoanalyst for a mental assessment.

However, for his records, he examined the girls to confirm that they were in good physical health before referring them back to the Reception desk. By then, the number of patients in the waiting room had increased to about fifty. Fortunately, they were given another number, No. 6 this time, and directed to a different waiting room to see the psychoanalyst.

Here, the mood was very different. The children seemed to be obedient and quiet. Some of them sat next to their parents and looked mostly at the ceiling, as if observing a football match, while some reacted suddenly as if they had seen Superman flying across the room. They were active with their hands and legs but were still very quiet. One boy was so silently active that he appeared to be taking part as a rebel in the Revolution all over again – all by himself, a one-boy army playing out in his mind.

The room was a school of mime. These children were all waiting for psychiatric assessment, and the reason they had been brought there to see the psychoanalyst was because they had shown some signs of unusual behaviour or mental deterioration. They seemed, however, to be the saner of the children in the two waiting rooms.

One should never be a doctor for selfish reasons, and this applies more so in Cuba where the training is hard, the hours are long, assignments are impossible and the pay is extremely low. The only recognition is that it is an honour to have served one's fellow man – and the Revolution. If the Hippocratic Oath does not mean very much elsewhere, it certainly means something in Cuba.

After waiting for another hour, Amelia and the girls were called in to see the psychoanalyst. By that time, Etna and Candelaria had become bored with waiting, having nothing to do but to observe the other children and their antics. They did not think about their school, but about their animal and bird friends and, when they eventually went in to see the psychoanalyst, they certainly had their feathered friends on their minds.

'Now, what is the problem?' asked Dr Caesaro.

Amelia related all that the girls had told her about the unusual occurrences and their dream concerning the African slaves.

'Did they both have the same dream?' asked the doctor.

'Yes, that's what they told their father and me – that they were both there in the same dream and they had met and spoken to the African slaves,' said Amelia.

'I must say that it is very unusual for two people to have the same dream. Are you girls still sure that you both had the same dream, and spoke to the African slaves?' asked Dr Caesaro.

'Yes, Doctor,' they both replied.

'Was this the first time you have had this dream or any similar dream?'

'It is the first time, so far as I am aware. They have often told us about their other dreams – about the birds and the animals which they call their friends,' said Amelia.

'It was the first time we saw the African slaves, Doctor,' said Etna.

'Did you know the African slave family or anyone who looked like them?' asked Dr Caesaro.

'No, we didn't know them,' said Etna.

'Did you have a lesson about slaves or African slaves in your school recently?'

'No, Doctor,' said both Etna and Candelaria.

'Did anyone tell you about the history of the African slaves?'

'No, Doctor, but we have heard people say that African slaves worked in the Valle a long time ago and they could not go to live somewhere else,' said Etna.

'Do you know where the African slaves came from?' asked Dr Caesaro.

'No, but we heard that they worked in the cane fields and were punished if they did not work – they were very sad,' said Etna.

'Have either of you read any stories about African slaves?'

'No, Doctor,' said Etna. 'We have only read in our story books about the animals of Africa, that's all.'

'Were the slave children punished too?' asked Candelaria.

Dr Caesaro found that he could not easily answer that last question, or thought it advisable not to volunteer an explanation.

It was, therefore, a convenient spot to bring that consultation to an end. He had heard what he wanted to know about the girls' dream and the conditions of their environment. He did not think that there was anything mentally abnormal about the girls. His opinion was that they must have overheard a conversation about African slaves at some time in the recent or distant past which they had never spoken about, but which had remained embedded in their subconscious and come to light only that night in their dreams.

He thought that Etna and Candelaria were no different from other young girls – intelligent, impressionable, quick to learn and enthusiastically inquisitive about life around them, to the extent that they had become closely attached to their environment and to the creatures which inhabited it. He was also of the opinion that the girls loved each other, liked being in each other's company and could easily mistake an activity as having been performed by one when it was actually performed or expressed by the other. His conclusion, therefore, was that the girls were normal, healthy human beings, and that their parents should not be unduly concerned about their state of mind.

It would seem that Dr Caesaro made a sound diagnosis. He concluded that the girls were not abnormal just because they had a bad dream. Being convinced of this, he did not enquire about the conversation with the African slaves and the task which the girls were asked to undertake. He was convinced that the details of that conversation were of no importance, since it was a fiction of the girls' imagination acted out in a dream. The girls' confirmation that they had spoken to the African family, as if it was real, was also of minor importance to his diagnosis.

Would the learned Doctor's diagnosis have been any different if the girls had said that they had dreamt of or seen the Virgin Mary or some other saintly personage? The question brings to mind the apparitions of Our Lady of Guadalupe in Mexico, Our Lady of

Lourdes in France and Our Lady of Fatima in Portugal. These examples did not come to Dr Caesaro's mind; otherwise he might have at least considered them in his final assessment. So it seems that one has to be very careful what one dreams about, for fear that one may be classified as a mental case or a saint.

Amelia did not know Dr Caesaro's age. She may have thought he was too young to understand the superstitions of the time, or that his medical training did not take such things into account as part of his education. He appeared young to her, perhaps about twenty-nine, but she was not surprised that he was so young to be fully qualified. The universities were producing doctors as fast as they could and exporting them to foreign countries which were in great need of such services. This was one of Fidel's more recent policies which the international community had criticised as a 'Revolution by other means'. But whatever the motive of this policy, it served as a means of international trade and an income earner for Cuba, and it also enhanced the reputation of Fidel Castro. As 'necessity is the mother of invention', it would seem that Fidel invented this policy in order to defeat the embargo imposed on the island, without the force of arms.

CHAPTER SIX

LA BOCA

The beach house was a small wooden house only a few metres from the beach. Bathers could be seen from the house, and the constant roar of the waves could be heard as the tide ebbed and flowed bringing its bubbled foam to be absorbed by the sand.

Even before Etna and Candelaria unpacked their bag, they asked for permission to play on the beach. Of course their parents agreed, while cautioning the girls not to go into the water but to wait until they could join them. The girls instantly changed into their red and white swim-suits and ran towards the beach. On their way, they passed near some sea crabs playing in the sand. When these saw the girls they continued to play but, as the girls approached, the crabs scuttled away into their burrow, disappearing and reappearing by the show of their pinnacled eyes – like periscopes – out of the burrow.

On the beach, the girls stopped to observe a couple of seagulls tearing away at their food – a dead fish which, in its fight for life, may have been washed up by the tide. There would have been more seagulls pecking at the fish, but they flew off as they saw the girls. Suddenly a black vulture swooped down and, enforcing its superiority, grabbed what remained of the fish and flew away.

It was still morning on a brilliant sunny Saturday and there were just a few people enjoying the air while walking along the beach. A few metres further down, there were two artists painting – sitting on stools and both facing east towards the horizon. The beach was quiet at that time of day, and one could imagine it even quieter during the working week or at unseasonal periods.

Cardenzo and Amelia joined their daughters and they all ran playfully into the sea. They splashed about and appeared to frighten the seagulls which had regained their former positions pecking at dead fish. The girls seemed so happy – a trip to the seaside is always

74

good mental and physical therapy, and it was wise of Mabelina to have suggested it.

The Martinez family bathed and played in the warm blue sea for over an hour, and then took a stroll down the beach towards the two artists who were still busy painting. Etna and Candelaria ran up to the artists to see what they were painting.

'Is that the sky and the sea?' asked Candelaria.

'Yes,' said the first artist.

'Why does his have so many brighter colours than yours?' asked Etna.

'Because we have different styles of painting. Don't you like my painting?'

'I don't know. You have not put much colour in it. And there are no birds in the sky,' said Etna.

'If you come back tomorrow you will see more colours and some birds in my painting, and then you can tell us what you think of it,' said the first artist.

'Both of you please stay there for a few minutes while I sketch your portrait. Yes, just like that,' said the second artist.

The second artist had begun to sketch the girls' portrait when they were summoned by their parents, but before they could leave, their photograph was taken in the pose in which they had been asked to remain. The artists continued painting as the Martinez family resumed their walk along the beach, splashing the water with their feet and trying to avoid the waves as they came in uneven proportions. They continued along the beach, holding hands, until they faded out of sight.

On their way back to the beach house, they again passed the two artists who were still absorbed in their painting. The girls waved to them and they waved back saying 'Hope you had a pleasant promenade!'

As they approached the house, the family saw two people coming along the beach towards them. They were walking close together and seemed to be enjoying each other's company. The girls recognised one of them as their Uncle Silvio, with a guitar slung over his shoulder. The other person was a young woman.

They greeted one another, and Silvio introduced his lady friend as Samara Agostina. He explained that he had known her for the past year, but he had kept this important information from Mabelina who, if she had known, would have enquired yet again about his plans, if any, to marry.

'I got Etna's letter yesterday and, since we were both free, I thought that we would surprise you,' said Silvio. 'I hope that you don't mind me inviting Samara'.

'Not at all. You are most welcome. It will be rough sleeping for you though, Silvio. You'll have to let Samara sleep on the couch and you will rough it on the floor,' said Amelia.

'We've just returned from a long walk along the beach and we are all very hungry. The sea air, you know, builds up the appetite. You must be hungry as well,' said Cardenzo.

'We haven't eaten since early breakfast, but we brought a few things – chicken and such. We will help you prepare lunch,' said Samara.

'Amelia has already prepared sandwiches. They will go well with your roast chicken' said Cardenzo. 'We did not know that you played the guitar.'

'I've been taking lessons for a few months and learning to sing as well. But it's not easy. I am not very good,' said Silvio.

'He plays reasonably well, although he is very shy,' said Samara.

'Shy for some things and brave for others,' said Cardenzo.

'Will you play for us later, Uncle?' asked Etna.

'Yes, but only a few songs which I already know.'

They had an enjoyable meal with the few items that were available to them. There were shortages, so they could not be extravagant when they felt like it. Their rations were controlled through their ration book, and to use up their supplies too quickly would mean that they would have to be extra economical for the rest of the week. But they were accustomed to shortages, and a few sandwiches and a chicken almost seemed a feast for six people. After all, they were on a two-day holiday. Meat was on the table and that made it exceptional.

After lunch, while Cardenzo, Amelia and Silvio chatted, the girls and Samara went back onto the beach to look at the sea and enjoy the heat of the sun. They played among the sand dunes, tidied up the beach of its debris brought up by the sea, and cooled their feet in the water. At every instant, the girls looked to see whether their parents and Silvio would join them on the beach but they did not. The girls would have concluded that their parents had a lot of family business to discuss with Silvio and therefore could not join them.

But the girls were in safe hands in the company of Samara. They stretched out on the beach intending to rest for a few minutes, but they must have fallen asleep for some time because, when they awoke, they observed the day had begun to turn grey. They sat up on the warm sand and listened to the breaking of the waves while, at the same time, trying to identify the flickering lights from both sides along the beach as the gradually encroaching night began to be lit up by the stars.

'Have you known Uncle long?' asked Etna.

'For about one year,' said Samara.

'Do you like my uncle?' asked Candelaria.

'Yes, I do.'

'Are you going to marry him then?' asked Candelaria.

'I think that your uncle is not the marrying kind.'

'What is 'not the marrying kind'?' asked Etna.

'He is a man who likes to live alone,' said Samara.

'But how can he have children if he lives alone?' asked Candelaria.

'That's a very good question. You must ask him that some day,' said Samara.

As the girls contemplated the next question to ask Samara, they heard the approaching sound of a single guitar playing. It was Silvio, and the tune was 'Dos Cosas'. When he reached them, the whole family sat on the beach and listened to Silvio's singing, while the dark was changing into several colours by the reflected light that came from across the ocean.

'You play very well, Uncle Silvio. Play another one for us,' said Etna.

The girls did not have to ask a second time. Uncle Silvio was there to entertain them and, at the same time, to practice a few songs. He played 'Olvido', 'Yolanda', 'Chan Chan' and 'Besame Mucho' which everyone enjoyed very much but, before he could finish, the girls were struggling to keep their eyes open and Cardenzo and Amelia took their leave and escorted the girls back to the beach house. Silvio and Samara remained on the beach, enjoying the cool night air and watching the lights in the houses along the beach go off one by one. When the beach was lit again by God's brief sun, it would be a new day.

The night had come too quickly for the girls. If they could have eradicated the night and let the day begin earlier, they would certainly have done so. But nature's natural beauty cannot be commanded, and everyone and everything in this world must be patient for life to evolve.

The sun rose in the east and the girls' window was facing the sun. They got dressed quickly, ran to the beach and stood at the edge of the tide as it came rolling onto the sand. They observed the small sea creatures searching for their early morning meal brought in by the sweeping tide. Small crabs were rushing to and from the water's edge carrying bits of food between their claws, and several miniature squid were desperately struggling to get back into the sea. Along the beach, numerous blue jelly-fish found themselves stranded by the receding tide. The seagulls were at breakfast and the girls could not fail to notice that small sea creatures do not live long in those parts.

At that early hour, around 7:00 a.m., there was nobody else on the beach except, surprisingly, the two artists, who appeared to have been painting for hours the colours of the horizon and the tranquil sea. The girls wondered at what hour they had risen. They stayed for a while, watching the artists from a distance, before they returned to the beach house for breakfast.

'Here are the early birds!' said Uncle Silvio.

'Good morning, Uncle and Samara,' said the girls.

'Do you always get up so early?' asked Samara.

'Oh yes, sometimes even before us. They like to feed the chicks and animals before they go to school,' said Amelia.

'Oh, my back! That floor was hard,' said Silvio.

'Don't be a baby, Silvio,' said Samara.

'You can't have a baby unless you are married, Uncle,' said Candelaria.

'I don't want a baby. Who said I want a baby?' asked Silvio.

They all looked at one another and did not pursue the question further. To do so would have precipitated a discussion on a subject that Silvio had avoided for some time.

After breakfast, Cardenzo, Silvio and the girls went to the beach to swim and to enjoy the last day of their break at the seaside. Amelia and Samara remained in the house to prepare lunch, and said that they would join the others later.

Cardenzo and Silvio sat on the beach while the girls played in the water in front of them. Cardenzo was happy to see that the girls were enjoying themselves and did not show any signs of stress. The seaside was having its therapeutic effect upon them and he wished that they could have stayed longer.

It was the first time, on this occasion, that the two brothers had an opportunity to speak privately to each other.

'Mama told me about your conversation with Señor Bronski,' said Cardenzo.

'I expect that she was disappointed in me,' said Silvio.

'She was really shocked to observe your outburst and was surprised at how much you have changed,' said Cardenzo. 'Why did you have to be so hard on Señor Bronski and critical of the Revolution?'

'That man really brings out the worst in me. But there were many things going on in my mind at the time. I had to let it out somehow and unfortunately he was the one there to receive it. I do not regret what I said to him but you are right, I should have been more discreet. I will have to apologise to Mama for my behaviour.'

'You'd better do that very soon because, regardless how conceited Señor Bronski is, he is considered a good friend of the family.'

'He said that you are a gentleman, which implies that I am not. I think that this was the only statement that he made which was correct. We have always been different in the ways that we deal with things,' said Silvio.

'I know you think that I don't know what's going on in our country. Some things are not right, but it is hopeless to speak about it or to try to convince people to do something about it. Since the

79

Revolution, the people have been hit by a wave of socialism so strong that we have seen objectors suffer the consequences of their words and actions. We have, therefore, kept silent and suffered in silence and, over the years, some have learnt how to survive better than others,' said Cardenzo.

'Do you think that we will ever get back our farm in Camaguey?' asked Silvio.

'Not if things continue as they are. But if change comes and our socialism is relaxed, then many things may happen. By change, I mean a better relationship with America and improved trade and investment,' said Cardenzo.

'Yes, I can see it now. For America to invest in the island, they may do so only on condition that all or some of their property is returned to them, or compensation is paid, or they are given guaranties for future investment,' said Silvio.

'That's right. If that happens and the Government goes much further and, in a climate of reconciliation, returns the properties of all the Cubans who left the island to go to Miami, then they will also have to do the same for everyone on the island whose property has been confiscated,' said Cardenzo.

'Then we could hope to get our farm back?'

'Yes,' said Cardenzo.

'What about all those people who boarded up their valuables in their houses in an attempt to conceal them from the authorities before going to Miami, or the property of the 'Boat People' who tried to flee Cuba and were caught or died in the attempt – would they or their families get their property back as well?' asked Silvio.

'I suppose so, if they or their relatives could prove ownership.'

'Then that is a great hope and wishful thinking which may never materialize. And if it means the destruction of socialism, I would prefer that they keep the farm and improve socialism,' said Silvio.

'I think we assume too much. We had better forget the farm for the immediate future, otherwise we will be disappointed,' said Cardenzo.

'As I see it, we would have to learn new skills – I mean the younger generation. We have been left out in the cold for so long that all the modern developments are unknown to us. The simple skill of repairing a modern car would create difficulties for us. We have developed ways of patching up our old vehicles but we would not be able to do that with the new technology,' said Silvio.

'But I don't think that most of our people would want that modern way of life anyway. We have grown up in our tranquil unstressed existence. We suffer less from heart attacks. Money and living in the fast lane would not be good for our people,' said Cardenzo.

'Well, just like socialism, change and progress would be forced down their throats. They would not be able to avoid it if our oil reserves are developed and more oil is discovered,' said Silvio.

'But, Silvio, do you really think that we have the possibility of developing an oil industry?'

'How big the industry would be no one knows as yet, but there seem to be more and more drilling operations appearing on the landscape in the west, near Pinar del Rio and the surrounding areas.'

'This I did not know. It seems to have been a well-kept secret,' said Cardenzo.

'If it was, it was not a secret for long. You can't keep the discovery of oil a secret. It's like a pregnant woman who wishes to keep her pregnancy a secret.'

'Well, if that's true, we are in for interesting times in Cuba,' said Cardenzo.

'I am not surprised that you don't know these things. Life in Havana is so different to other parts of the country. It is a more forward-looking place, as you would expect the capital to be. Embargo or no embargo, Havana still has to keep in touch with the outside world. Don't forget that Cuba still has her embassies operating in many foreign countries.'

'Are you telling me that Havana is involved with the outside world more that the rest of the island realises?'

'Yes, and that is one of the reasons why *Habaneros* appear to be doing better than the people in the countryside. It is also not in the Government's interest to inform the people of these things.'

'So us country people are kept in the dark?'

'Yes,' said Silvio. 'It is the nature of governments, leaders and rulers to have their ideologies and policies – the reasons why they won an election or had a revolution. If they stick doggedly to those reasons they would not have contact with anyone with opposing views outside their country. They, therefore, have to sacrifice some of their principles in order to co-exist or even to survive.'

'Do you think that the Catholic Church could be important again in Cuba?' asked Cardenzo.

'I think so. The Comandante now allows them to celebrate Mass in the Cathedral, and don't forget that the Pope visited us just a few years ago,' said Silvio. 'That is certainly a change in the Comandante's policy. He used to be so anti-Catholic because he believed that the Church had a great influence on the people and was a force against the Revolution. He did not want any opposition from them, although he himself was a Catholic.'

'I believe that he is still a Catholic,' said Cardenzo.

'I don't doubt it. I remember when the Pope visited Cuba and the Comandante gave his speech of welcome. The Pope was sitting next to him while he did so, his hand supporting his head in contemplation, listening to the Comandante. That photograph appeared in the newspapers. By the Pope's expression, he could have been saying: 'What is this man going on about?' or, 'How long do I have to bear this?' said Silvio.

'We have been speculating for years about the future of our country yet, in the end, we are still experiencing hard times. We had better concentrate on more immediate matters, such as your apology to Mama,' said Cardenzo.

'I shall apologise, but I am not so worried about that conversation. I am more concerned about other matters. You know, there is something that I wanted to tell you before, but I did not want to involve you and the family in my business.'

'What business is that, brother?'

'It's not a 'business' really. It's just that I have not been acting right, and that has been bothering me for some time now,' said Silvio.

'Are you in love? Are you thinking of getting married?' asked Cardenzo, impatiently. 'I would not be surprised, Samara seems a nice girl'.

'That may be part of it. Eventually I may marry her because she is very *simpatica* and, of all the girls I have known, I think I like her the best.'

'Have you discussed it with her? Did Candelaria overhear your discussion with Samara speaking about babies?'

'No! I have not spoken to her about it. But that is not what I wanted to tell you, although what I want to tell you may affect any ideas of marriage,' said Silvio.

'Is it something very serious then?'

'It may or may not be. You see, for the past two years, I have been stealing a few of the factory's tobacco leaves and making cigars to sell myself. No one can tell the difference between the factory cigars and my own. I have all the equipment to pass off the cigars as if made by the factory. So I make extra money by selling them to certain buyers at a greatly reduced price.'

'But this is dangerous! If you are caught, don't you realise ...?'

'Yes, I know. I would be imprisoned and greatly dishonoured.'

'Well, why don't you stop?' asked Cardenzo, keeping a watchful eye on the girls.

'That is exactly what I have decided. I want to stop completely and 'give to Fidel what is due to Fidel', but it is not as easy as that. You see, the people who buy my cigars may put pressure on me to continue, and they could be very vicious if they want to.'

'Have they threatened you?'

'Not directly, but they have a reputation for violence.'

'They must realise that, if the authorities find out, they too would be in trouble,' said Cardenzo.

'Of course they know that, but they would expect me to keep my mouth shut if I am caught.'

'I can see how this could affect any future wedding plans you may have. It is no good getting married when, at any moment, you may be sent to jail.'

'So you see my predicament?'

'Yes. You have found yourself in the quicksand and the more you try to escape, the deeper you sink,' said Cardenzo.

'I have been thinking about this problem for some time, and I have come to the conclusion that there is only one way out of it for me,' said Silvio.

'What is that?'

'I think that I would have to feign sickness and go off on sick leave for a few weeks, and then eventually resign from the factory as a result of ill health some time later.'

'But then what would you do for a living?'

'I would try the entertainment business, playing the guitar and singing. I could make quite a good living here,' said Silvio.

'Is that the reason you took up playing the guitar?'

'Yes. Do you think that could be a good way out of my problems?'

'Well, it seems that you have been thinking about this for some time. Your 'personal customers' shouldn't have any suspicion that you deliberately resigned. You would, of course, have to move away from Havana and live in another town.'

'I never thought that I would have to leave Havana, but I can see the sense of it. I suppose I could go to Santiago or any other big town, or even go abroad, if I am allowed,' said Silvio.

'You may not have to go abroad voluntarily. If they do not imprison you, they may deport you as a traitor of the Revolution,' warned Cardenzo.

'I must put my plan into effect immediately.'

'You should.'

'Please do not tell Mama about my problems. She would be so distressed and will worry on my behalf,' said Silvio.

At that moment, Amelia and Samara arrived to join Cardenzo and Silvio on the beach. They had prepared lunch and were ready to enjoy the soothing caresses of the water, free from domestic distraction. They did not say anything to the two brothers, but went over to Etna and Candelaria, who were anxiously waiting for their father to finish his conversation with their uncle so they could go into the sea.

'Come on girls!' said Amelia, and the two girls happily ran into the water with Amelia and Samara. They splashed about with such excitement that the two brothers decided to join them and take part in the fun.

After they had swum and played in the sea for some time, the two girls walked across to the two artists who were still painting in the place where the girls had previously seen them.

'Hello girls. How are you today?' the first artist greeted them.

'Haven't you finished painting that picture yet?' asked Candelaria.

'No. We will have to finish painting it at home,' said the first artist.

'You have more colours to put in?' asked Etna.

'Yes, many more,' said the first artist.

'Where is your home, Señor?' asked Etna

'In England,' said the first artist. 'And what is your name?'

'My name is Etna, and this is my sister, Candelaria.'

'Well, I am Donald, and he is Leonard,' said the first artist.

'Have you finished painting the picture of us as yet, Leonard?' asked Etna.

'I have started your portrait, but it's not finished as yet. When it is finished, I will have to post it to you, if you can give me your address.'

The girls gave their full names and address which was noted in Leonard's sketch-book.

'Where is England?' asked Etna.

'Across the sea. Maybe some day you will travel there and come to visit us. When I send you the portrait, I will also give you my full address,' said Leonard.

'It would be nice to travel on a big boat across the sea,' said Candelaria.

'Or you can travel by aeroplane. It's faster,' said Leonard.

'I will tell Mama and Papa that I would like to visit there,' said Candelaria.

'That would be nice, but I expect that she would say: 'Not for many years – until you have grown up',' said Leonard.

'Do you need a lot of money to go there?' asked Etna.

'I think so,' said Leonard.

'Then we cannot visit England because we do not have a lot of money,' said Etna.

'Do you girls go to school?' asked Donald.

'Yes,' replied Candelaria.

'Then you must ask your teacher to show you where England is on a map of the world,' said Donald.

It was one of those encounters, where passing strangers meet for an instant and never expect to meet again. That was the opinion of Donald and Leonard, but the two girls, of course, spoke about the future in such a way as if it was a certainty.

In life there is no certainty of what the future holds for adventurers such as Donald and Leonard for whom, in a country like Cuba, all the beauty is stored up in their memories and in their paintings to be called upon and reflected on in their golden years. Etna and Candelaria were at the other end of the age spectrum, and would no doubt come to look upon the encounter as a faint shadow in their memories. It was just by chance that Donald and Leonard had met Etna and Candelaria, the 'purest in the land', although they did not know this and thought of them only as charming and pleasant little girls.

But had Leonard unintentionally drawn the girls' attention to the disadvantages of their status – the fact that they did not have enough money to travel to England if they wanted to, and that they were poor, when all the time the girls had believed that they lived the most perfect lives – never wanting more, never envying others and that they already had all that life could give and were happy, even though they were poor?

Recognising the possible damage, Leonard was relieved when the subject was changed to 'school' and 'maps'. Donald and Leonard packed up their painting materials, folded their easels and told the girls that they were off to lunch. They wished the girls a happy holiday and farewell, saying 'We will not forget you'.

Etna and Candelaria walked back to the beach house and rejoined their parents. They all went into the house for their lunch. It was the last meal that they would have at the seaside because, after lunch, they would return to the beach, have their last swim and, at five o'clock, take the bus back to the Valle de los Ingenios.

'What were the artists saying to you, Etna?' asked Amelia.

'They said that they live in England and that they would post the picture they painted of us when it is finished,' said Etna.

'How far is England, Mama?' asked Candelaria.

'It is very far from Cuba. I will show you in the World Atlas tomorrow,' said Amelia.

'Will we be able to visit there one day, Mama?' asked Etna.

'I hope that in the future, when you are old enough, you will be able to travel anywhere in the world,' said Amelia.

'Have you visited England, Samara?' asked Etna.

'No, my dear, I cannot afford to travel.'

'Why can't people afford to travel?' asked Candelaria.

'Because some people have money and some do not,' answered Cardenzo.

'But why do some people have money and we don't?' asked Etna.

'Good question, Etna! Now let me hear your Papa answer that,' said Silvio.

'The answer is not difficult. Some people do not have money because the Revolution is still young and we have to work very hard for it to survive. When it has survived and continued doing well, we will work for lots of money,' said Cardenzo.

'But would lots of money make us happy, Papa?' asked Etna.

'Good question again, Etna. You are an intelligent girl. People have been trying to answer that question for ages,' said Silvio.

'People do not need lots of money to be happy, Etna. If people have the necessary things of life – like food, water, fresh air, a simple place to live, some liberty and peace and the lovely beaches and seas of our island – they can live a happy life. They could be very happy,' said Cardenzo.

'But we already have all that, Papa, so we must be happy,' said Etna.

'How thoughtful you are, Etna, but your Papa has left out one important thing – envy. If people want what their neighbours or friends have, or want more than what is essential to life, then they would not be happy,' said Silvio.

'But Candelaria and I do not want more. We already have our Mama and Papa, our Grandma, Gallina, Dulcina and the chicks,' said Etna.

'And what about me, your Uncle?'

'Yes, and you too, Uncle Silvio,' said Etna.

'And you have me too,' added Samara.

'But I want to have a hen for Dulcina so that we can have some more chicks and some eggs,' exclaimed Candelaria, to everyone's amusement.

Cardenzo deliberately did not inform Silvio of the recent 'happenings' in the Valle. He should have, but he knew that Silvio would have been concerned for the girls' welfare. Silvio had his own problems and Cardenzo thought it better not to get him involved in the affairs of the Valle, which could, perhaps, later come to his rescue as a means of escape from Havana should he need it. But even to do that would have placed the Martinez family at risk, since everyone in the Valle would know if a newcomer was residing there.

They said their good-byes as they took the bus back to the Valle de los Ingenios. When they arrived there, Mabelina was waiting for them. She embraced them affectionately, and immediately enquired whether their short break at the seaside was a success. Without any hesitation, Cardenzo was able to answer positively – believing that the girls had forgotten their bad dreams and that such dreams would not occur again.

When Etna and Candelaria went to bed that night, they thought of the sea, the sand, the sound of the waves, the artists painting on the beach, and the happy times they had spent with their parents, Uncle Silvio and Samara.

The girls slept well that night, and for many nights after their weekend at the seaside. Their parents were very pleased that they appeared to have settled back into their normal routine. For Cardenzo and Amelia, 'sleeping well' meant that the girls did not dream about the African slaves. They were aware that everyone dreams, but many of those dreams may not be remembered by the dreamer. If they are remembered, they are usually not of any importance so as to prompt concern or investigation.

CHAPTER SEVEN

APPARITIONS – SECOND VISIT

Yes, the girls dreamt, and they continued to dream about their weekend at the beach and the wonderful time they had there. But there was one constantly recurring dream that followed through to the end. They dreamt that they were gliding across the ocean to a foreign land. The ocean was always calm and silvery, especially at night when the moon was full and bright. It was like a fairy-tale. No fear or pain existed – only a deep sense of pleasure as they travelled effortlessly across the ocean. They saw the colours of the rainbow, as well as colours which the rainbow subtly possesses but which cannot normally be detected by the naked eye. Their journey never seemed to end until the girls were awake at the first appearance of the sun.

That was not a dream that the girls thought should be reported to their parents. It was a dream of the type that people have every day. If their parents were told of this dream, they would have dismissed it as of no importance.

One night, the girls continued to have the same dream that they were smoothly gliding across the ocean. But, before they could enter the colours of the rainbow, strong winds started to blow, the sea became rough, and the silvery colour of the ocean turned to blue. They heard cries of anguish everywhere and then they became afraid. Their fear did not last long, however, for the ocean quickly turned calm again as they heard the sound of familiar voices and then saw the appearance of familiar faces – faces which they had never forgotten since their first encounter – the faces of the African slaves.

'Etna, Candelaria, have you forgotten us?' asked Grandfather Abufera.

'We have not forgotten you,' said Etna.

'We have been waiting too long for the 'purest' to be our saviour, and now that we have found you, we know that you will be true,' said Abufera.

'What are your names?' asked Candelaria.

'We told you that our names are Luther, Rose, Toto and Daisy, and my name is Dominic, but those were the names given to us by our master, Angel Montevideo, because he wanted to destroy our identity and heritage and hide us from the world that we lived in and from the future. Our birth names are Utatambo Abufera, who is myself; Ubero Tatimo, who is my son here with me; Puranduma, my son's wife; Tatantumbo, my grandson, and Claratuma, who is my granddaughter.

We were shifted from world to world and everywhere the fury burned severe and unimaginable. You must find our remains and bury us in holy ground, if we are to be found and to live again in tranquil spirit. Go to the end of the Lane and look to the bend in the track which took the wagons to the shore and then look no more. In the water-well there dwell a hundred years of tears – soaked in blood among other Spirits of the Earth. Cleanse all souls and restore them to their proper place for we are in a race against time to defeat the Evil One. Farewell our angels,' said Abufera.

'Farewell, and we promise,' said Etna and Candelaria.

The blue of the ocean evaporated and all was calm and silvery again. The girls slept on, motionless and uninterrupted from the time they had gone to bed. Again their dream had come to them and they were passive recipients of its message – all that the mind goes through as slumber extinguishes consciousness. But to Etna and Candelaria, the intensity of the dream was too strong and could not be ignored. They thought that this time they must fulfil their promise.

At dawn, the girls woke their parents to tell them that they had seen the African family again.

'Are you sure, my dears?' asked Amelia.

'Yes, Mama, we saw them as we see you and Papa now,' said Etna.

'Yes, it's true,' said Candelaria.

'What did they say?' asked Amelia.

'They were sad and asked if we had forgotten them,' said Candelaria.

'They said that we should look to the bend in the track and we will find the water-well,' said Etna.

'Don't get too excited girls! There is no bend in the track,' said Cardenzo.

Cardenzo was surprised that the dream had recurred, but he knew that this time he had to take the girls seriously and examine what the African family was asking them to do.

'The African family said that their remains are in a water-well and you should look to the bend in the track?' Cardenzo confirmed. 'I will have a look after breakfast. But first, I must speak to the Administrator of the Manaca Estate to find out if there was ever a bend in the track or a water-well at the end of the Lane. I will have to report absent from work today in order to get to the bottom of your dreams. But both of you must go to school while I look into the matter.'

CHAPTER EIGHT

THE SEARCH

After breakfast, Cardenzo went down to the rail-track at the end of the Lane to confirm that there was no 'bend in the track' and therefore no water-well, before going to the Manaca Mansion to make further enquiries. He walked along the section of the track that ran between the huts in a straight line from west to east. It was overhung by banana trees and covered with overgrown vegetation, indicating that it had not been used for a long time.

Cardenzo could not find a bend in the track, neither was there a water-well or any indication of one. If there was a water-well, it would have been covered up by the thick vegetation or the years of accumulated soil which had sprouted wild plants and flowers along the track. Although this section of the rail-track had been disused for many years, the authorities had not thought it necessary to remove it. They may have considered it a waste of money to do so, since the track had served only the former sugar-mills and plantations in the Valle. The sugar industry had declined now, and, since the Valle did not attract other industries, this section of the track had been forgotten.

As Cardenzo searched for the bend with a water-well, he saw Señor Virgilio Tomasas, the old man who was known as 'Señor Green Tree' or 'The Invisible Man'. He lived in one of the huts on the south side of the rail-track. He was probably about 80 years of age, although no one knew exactly how old he was. He was a strange man – a loner – and, on first meeting him, one was guaranteed not to like him. But then again, those who met him for the first time would not understand his character or spend a little time getting to know him.

Señor Tomasas had lived in the Valle since the Revolution, having joined the Rebels when they came down from the Sierra

Maestra. He had excelled himself in the Uprising and would have been chosen for promotion in the army of the New Order, but he had done his fair share of killing and was sent instead to work on the farms of Sancti Spiritus, before being reallocated to the Valle de los Ingenios. Some people suggested that he was mentally affected by all the killing that he had done in the Uprising, and that had changed him into an unpleasant person. He had never married, and nobody had ever seen him smile since he came to live in the Valle.

He always wore his green outfit – green shirt, trousers, gardening boots and even a green hat – which made him almost invisible among his green surroundings. He had a small beard and a scar on the right side of his face which he may have received while fighting in the Revolution. Everywhere he went, he carried his machete with him. His appearance was rather sinister, and that may have been the reason why people did not make an effort to try to get to know him or to ask him about his activities in the Uprising. He was not a man who could be asked such questions.

His machete was used for cultivating his vegetable garden and keeping the surroundings of his neighbourhood free from weeds and intruding plants. Maybe it was also the aggressive way in which he used his machete that caused people to think that he was a dangerous man and to shun him. But here was a man who was only being himself and living the way he chose – wrapped up in the past and keeping his thoughts to himself. This would have been a difficult task to achieve, and would have been found peculiar by the residents in the circumstances of Cuban life, so long as politics were not openly discussed. One could quite reasonably say that he was a lonely man. But Señor Tomasas seemed to thrive in his loneliness, although no one knew whether he was a happy man or not.

He knew the Valle well, and all who lived there. He knew Etna and Candelaria and would have seen them every day, playing in the fields and along the rail-track. He would have kept an eye on them to see that they did not get into trouble. He was, in many ways, their unofficial silent protector.

Often, even when they did not see him, the girls could sense whenever he was in the vicinity. Their 'seventh' sense and the behaviour of the wild birds and animals would have alerted them to his presence. And, if by chance they did see him, they would speak to him kindly, for they may have detected a strange sadness in his countenance. Etna and Candelaria seemed to be the exceptional few people who were not afraid of him for, on many occasions, he would speak to them and advise them to make their way home when they were late, as their parents would be anxious about them.

'*Buen dia*, Señor Tomasas,' said Cardenzo.

'*Buen dia*, Señor Martinez.'

'I am looking for a water-well that was supposed to be along this rail-track near the end of the Lane, but I just can't find it. Do you know if there was ever a water-well around here?' asked Cardenzo.

'Let me see. A well, you say? A water-well, along this rail-track? No, I have never seen one – not in all the time I have been here. Are you sure it was at the end of the Lane near the rail-track?'

'I was told that it could be found at the bend in the track, but, so far as I can see, there is no bend in the track,' said Cardenzo.

'Well, there is a bend in the track where the line from Trinidad separates to the north.'

'No, that's not it. I was told that it could be found near the end of the Lane,' said Cardenzo.

'But there is no bend in the track and no water-well there – not to my knowledge. Where did you get your information from?' asked Señor Tomasas.

'I will tell you another time, after I have made some more enquiries at the Mansion House. They should know.'

'OK. Good luck!' said Señor Tomasas, swishing his machete at the overgrown grass as he walked on. He may have thought that if Cardenzo did not want to tell him from where he had got his information that was his right. He was not a man to delve further, for he also did not want anyone to enquire into his own affairs. The way he lived his life, he gave the impression of a man living with an important secret who was determined to keep that secret to himself at all costs.

Cardenzo was cautious not to tell Señor Tomasas from where he had got his information about the water-well. He did not want to spread the news of the girls' dreams so as to cause alarm and excitement, or for anyone to think that his daughters may be hallucinating. Too much attention focussed upon the girls would have distracted them from their studies and exposed them to ridicule by their peers.

Cardenzo was convinced that the girls had told him the truth about their dreams but, after speaking to Señor Tomasas, he was beginning to have some doubts that the water-well ever existed. If Señor Tomasas did not know, then it was unlikely that anyone else would know. On the other hand, Señor Tomasas had lived in the Valle only since the time of the Revolution – almost 50 years before – and it was unlikely that he would have known the history of the Valle prior to that time.

So, in order to satisfy himself that the girls were telling the truth or, indeed, if their story was merely a fantasy of their imagination, Cardenzo had to investigate the matter at the Manaca Mansion House where some record would have been kept about the history of the Valle de los Ingenios.

The Mansion House and its associated activities – tourism and the general management of the Valle – were run by an Administrator, Señor Rafael Guerra, who was a supporter of the Revolution. He was also Head of the Works Committee for the Valle and, therefore, accountable to the Minister of the Interior and Labour Affairs. He knew all the workers and their families who lived and worked in the Valle, and was well acquainted with Cardenzo.

Cardenzo enquired from Señor Guerra whether he could tell him if there was a water-well at the end of the Lane near the rail-track at the rear of the Iznaga Tower.

'Why do you want to know this information?' asked Señor Guerra.

Cardenzo realised that it was not a question he could ask the Administrator without giving him an explanation. He was, therefore, compelled to tell him, in detail, about the girls' dreams and what had been asked of them, and to say that he was also concerned for the welfare of his daughters. Cardenzo became emotional, and when he explained the girls' dreams he appeared distressed.

Señor Guerra took the normal line that everyone has dreams at night – some are pleasant while others may be unpleasant. He did not believe in the superstitions of the island, but he was aware that some people were influenced by them and that certain sects, such as *Santeria*, are sought out to obtain their charms and mysterious magical incantations. He believed that these things were to be tolerated, only so long as they do no harm.

'Your daughters are very young and, therefore, would have great imagination, and that imagination would be reflected in their dreams,' said Señor Guerra.

'But, Señor, that's what I thought when they first told me of their dreams. I could expect both of them to have flights of fantasy, but not the same fantasies at the same time. My girls are honest girls and they would always tell their parents the truth,' said Cardenzo.

'I must admit that is a strange occurrence – both of them having the same dream at the same time.'

Señor Guerra thought about the coincidences of the dreams and, although he was not superstitious, he could not find a rational explanation for such an occurrence. He went to his bookshelves and took up a book on the life of Fidel Castro. He flicked through its pages, paused and read:

'*Daytime bravado, machismo, the mystique of the much loved pistol, all languished in the dark, however, when dangers to a young boy growing up in Oriente were not human but were from another world. Galicians warned their children of the 'Holy Company of Lost Souls' dressed in black and doomed to wander the world at night until they could catch some unsuspecting stranger's eye and require him to take their place. Afro-Cuban and Haitian babies imbibe with their mothers' milk the folk tales of spirits moving about in the hours of darkness. At these times old men prudently stayed awake, telling stories until the cock crowed. Cubans of all social classes, even medical doctors and educators, protected themselves from nocturnal airs, covering their noses and mouths to prevent the mischievous spirits from entering and doing them harm. And uneducated Cubans slept with their heads covered and the doors and windows tightly closed.*' [*Fidel Castro* by Robert E. Quirk]

'You see, even the Comandante believes in superstitious occurrences,' said Cardenzo.

'Yes, but not everyone does.'

Señor Guerra was troubled by the constant advocates of the unknown but, although he generally dismissed such occurrences, he could not disprove their existence. However, in this case, he thought he might be able to prove the fantasy of the girls' dreams once and for all.

'Come with me, Cardenzo. Let's investigate this matter and check the facts in the archives,' he said, leading the way to another room.

Geological and architectural books and survey maps were consulted.

'Ah, here it is! The *Government Survey Maps of the Valle de los Ingenios, 1875 to 1910*. Let's see – the railway was built in 1875. Now what does this map show? *Dios mio!* There is a bend in the track and a water-well is shown.'

'So the girls were telling the truth all the time. I knew that they would not lie to me. They are good girls,' said Cardenzo.

'Now let's see when the water-well was built. Ah, it says here that the existing water-well was constructed in 1875, in order to service the steam locomotive that ran between the sugar-mills, and that it was sealed over in 1910, after that section of the railway track fell into disuse. The bend in the track was a branch line that joined it to the main line. That part of the track was taken up when the locomotive stopped running and the water-well was abandoned. Everything is shown clearly here on this official Survey Map. I did not believe it, but your daughters' information was absolutely correct,' said Señor Guerra.

'It seems then that they really did see those apparitions of African slaves,' said Cardenzo.

'It would seem so. I just do not know. My beliefs are shaken. It also appears that there was a water-hole there long before 1875 – the source of it may have come from the Sierra del Escambray. I cannot see any indication of it here on this map. I shall have to check later to see if it is recorded on other maps. But now that we know where the 'bend in the track' is located, we will have to excavate the area to find the water-well.'

'How soon could we start excavating?' asked Cardenzo.

'Tomorrow morning at eight. I will get some men and digging equipment by then,' said Señor Guerra. 'You can take tomorrow off from your usual work and give us a hand as well'.

'Yes, I certainly want to be there,' said Cardenzo.

Señor Guerra was sixty-one years of age. He was one of those citizens who had taken advantage of the education made available to him by the Revolution. He was an intelligent man and had worked in various jobs around the island on behalf of the Government. His judgement was always accepted as sound and, over the years, he had been promoted to senior positions of responsibility, finally being placed as Administrator in charge of the Valle de los Ingenios.

But today, his intelligence was challenged. If he had not seen the facts documented, he would certainly not have believed the girls' story. He was thrown off-balance by the discovery, because he had lived all his life believing that the island's superstitions were exaggerated stories of fantasies. He was not influenced by Fidel's own beliefs. He may have thought that Fidel, being a politician, had his own reasons for continuing the belief in superstitions, but being a strong supporter of the Revolution, he could not openly voice an opinion to Cardenzo that was opposed to that of the Comandante.

It was the discovery of the recorded facts that made Señor Guerra doubt his long-held beliefs. He was determined to discover the truth or falsity of the girls' story. Unless he investigated that story thoroughly, he could not make a declaration or inform the Government of such matters, for fear that they might think that he was going out of his mind.

CHAPTER NINE

THE EXCAVATION

Promptly at eight the next morning, Señor Guerra, Cardenzo and five farm workers left the Manaca Mansion House with machetes and digging equipment and walked down the Lane to the dirt track behind the Iznaga Tower. At the rail-track, Señor Guerra consulted the Survey Map and went to the spot where the bend in the track was indicated. They observed that the rail-track was not continuous as everyone had thought. The track was joined in several places, which indicated that it had been previously taken up and realigned. They agreed that this was the most obvious place where a diversion of the line would have been made, or a branch line commenced or, as the girls had said, 'a bend in the track' took place.

There was no obvious sign of a water-well where it had been indicated on the Survey Map. They therefore decided to excavate the area along the side of the track, where the bend was indicated on the map. They cut back the overgrown grass and shrubs and uprooted several small trees. Then the five men and Cardenzo cleared the soil and piled it up on the other side of the track.

After clearing the site and digging for over an hour, one of the workmen struck a concrete base about one and a half metres from the rail-track. A pneumatic drill and compressor were sent for in order to break the concrete.

The men took the opportunity to have a rest but, while they did so, they talked with trepidation about what they expected to discover when the concrete was broken into. Knowing the purpose of the excavation, wild superstitious thoughts went through their minds. They believed that the remains of the dead should not be disturbed in their place of burial, and that all those who interfere with or disturb them would inherit a turbulent life and all the evils of an unknown world.

But the farm workers could not refuse to obey the orders of Señor Guerra, since he was a senior member of the Committee and their livelihood depended on his good report.

When the pneumatic drill was brought to the site, none of the workmen volunteered to be the first to start breaking the concrete area. Seeing the men's reluctance, Cardenzo took the drill and began to break the concrete. This proved to be very thick – more than half a metre deep. One of the workers was called by Señor Guerra to relieve Cardenzo, and he continued the drilling until he had made a small hole. Then a third man took over and expanded the hole in the concrete. They discovered that they had unearthed what appeared to be a well and it was filled to the top with soil.

One man was sent into the well to excavate the soil. The men took turns in digging and removing the soil and, with a constructed rope and bucket, they dug deeper into the well. When they had dug down to about five metres, they noticed that human bones were mixed in with the soil. One of the workmen cried out: *'Que Dios nos perdone! Este sitio esta maldito!'* ['May God forgive us! This place is damned.'] Everyone realised that they had found what they were looking for.

They continued to excavate, and hundreds of human bones were dug up. As they dug deeper into the well, a strange smell pervaded the place. The men had to cover their mouths and noses, and they proceeded to excavate the soil at a much faster rate in order to complete the digging quickly, so as not to be exposed too long to the noxious air.

During that afternoon, the news of Etna's and Candelaria's dream had spread throughout the Valle, and a number of spectators gathered to observe what was going on. The workman's exclamation instilled them with fear, and the sight of so many human bones made them realise that a massacre had taken place in the Valle.

'It must have been a massacre because otherwise the bones would not have been in the well,' said First Spectator.

'But who is responsible?' asked Second Spectator.

'That depends when it took place. Are those responsible still alive to be held accountable? It does not seem to be recent,' said Third Spectator.

'That's true. It must have happened some time in the past because we never knew there was a well here,' said First Spectator.

'So no one would be held responsible?' asked Second Spectator.

'The question is how did the girls know about the well and the people buried there? Did they really see and speak to African slaves? Did they see an apparition?' asked Third Spectator.

'And, if so, why were they chosen?' asked Second Spectator.

'It all seems very strange to me. When you hear stories like this, you put it down to superstition. But to actually see the reality of one's dream come true makes you wonder whether there may be more to superstitious happenings than we would like to believe,' said Third Spectator.

'You are right. How could you deny what is happening here today?' said First Spectator.

'But why were the girls chosen to make such a discovery?' asked Second Spectator.

'I suppose we may never know,' said First Spectator.

'I think the girls were chosen instead of an adult, because no one would have believed an adult,' said Third Spectator.

'Look out! Here comes Señor Tomasas,' said the First Spectator.

The workmen placed all the remains they had dug up into wooden boxes, ready to be taken up to the Mansion House to await further investigation. It seemed that the well had been dry for many years. The underground river which may have come from the Sierra del Escambray must have naturally diverted its course, thereby leaving the well to dry up and be abandoned.

Had the massacre taken place before or after the river changed its course and the well was abandoned, or while the well was still functioning for the use of the locomotives when sugar-cane was king, and perhaps also being used by the local residents? If this latter was the case, it would have been a diseased well and an epidemic would surely have broken out at the time. There were many questions to be answered and investigations to be made in order to put straight the history of the Valle.

Meanwhile, a local reporter had got wind of the excavation and turned up on the scene. He represented the *Rebelde* newspaper, and this story was certainly out of the ordinary for him – different from

101

politics and the achievements of the Revolution, on which he was usually required to write. This was a story in which everyone on the island would be interested. It addressed the questions of many, while others might be more sceptical and confused since they did not believe in miracles or magic. The reporter spoke to some of the spectators, making notes and taking photographs.

One of those spectators was Señor Tomasas, who had earlier in the day seen when the excavation had started but not intervened, preferring to observe quietly from the shrubbery. But as the excavation continued with bones being unearthed and the crowd getting larger, he drew closer to see what was being discovered. He seemed disturbed by the sight of the bones. Listening to the comments of the spectators, he felt angry that the excavation and the girls' story had drawn the attention of the public to the Valle.

The reporter approached him and asked: 'Señor, did you know that there was a well here?'

'No.'

'How long have you lived in the Valle?'

'Nearly fifty years,' said Señor Tomasas. 'And all these people should not be here. This is a quiet place where people should be left alone.'

'Don't you think that this is an interesting story? Why do you resent the people being here?' asked the reporter.

'The dead should be left to bury the dead. Why interfere with things which took place long ago, and disrupt the lives of the people in this Valle?'

'But Señor, how do you know these things happened long ago and not more recently?' asked the reporter.

'I have said enough,' said Señor Tomasas, as he walked away through the shrubbery swinging his machete in his hand and taking his thoughts with him. Did the likelihood of a massacre bring back bad memories to him?

The reporter found him to be an interesting character but did not pursue him further. Instead, he spoke to another resident to try and find out more about Señor Tomasas' personal life.

'Señor Tomasas? All one knows is that his name is Señor Virgilio Tomasas and he served in the Revolutionary army. He is not a pleasant person,' said the man.

'Has he been living here long?' asked the reporter.

'Too long for our liking.'

The reporter thought that there was something strange about Señor Tomasas and he would have liked to learn more, but that would have to be enquired into another day.

The girls' story was a fascinating one and he asked Señor Guerra, the Administrator, to make a statement.

'We have excavated this well on the basis of information received from Señor Cardenzo Martinez. We found the location of the well from official Survey Maps in our archives. It is true that the origin of the information was derived from Señor Martinez's two young daughters who informed their father that they were told in their dreams that there were people buried in the well. Without that information, we would never have discovered these human remains. It seems that a tragedy has taken place here. I do not want to draw any conclusions about it at the moment. The remains will be sent to the Forensic Pathologist's Department in Havana for identification and report. Until then, I cannot say more,' said Señor Guerra.

While all this was going on, the girls were totally oblivious of the commotion that was taking place in the Valle. They were dutifully engaged in school work and with their school friends. Although they knew that their father was going to make enquiries about the water-well, they were not overly excited about it. Their demeanour was calm. They believed what the African family had told them, and they expected the inevitability of the discovery of their remains. They took everything in their stride as if the encounter and request of the African family was normal – just like an ordinary day at school.

They had not discussed their dreams with their teachers or their school friends. Their father had told them not to do so and they followed his instructions faithfully. They did not fear the encounter in their dreams, believing that there was no difference between dreams and reality. If they saw people in their dreams and spoke to them they believed that was part of life, just as if they were speaking to their friends on the telephone – although they did not have one –

or like writing a letter and then receiving a reply. They could not see the immediate transportation of their conversation or message by these means, yet they believed it and everyone accepted it as normal everyday life.

As the workmen completed their work at the well and were placing a cover over it, one of the onlookers shouted: 'There they are!', and everyone rushed up the Lane towards Etna and Candelaria who were just returning from school. Cardenzo managed to get ahead of the crowd, but as the people reached the girls, they plied them with questions.

'Did you really see the Spirits?'

'How did they appear to you?'

'Weren't you afraid?'

'How many Spirits did you see?'

'Did the Spirits tell you why they chose you?'

Cardenzo tried his best to protect his daughters from the crush and prevented them from answering any questions. The people were, of course, curious to know more of the girls' dreams. For their part, Etna and Candelaria were taken by surprise, and were astonished by the size of the crowd. From the questions the girls were asked, they assumed that the public had been told about their dreams, although they could not begin to anticipate the extent of the day's discoveries and the people's excitement. But the girls were not afraid of or intimidated by the crowd. Cardenzo was more concerned that some harm may befall them. As he was taking the girls back to their home, the reporter shouted out his request for an interview.

'Señor Martinez, I am from the *Rebelde* newspaper. Can I speak to your daughters?'

Cardenzo contemplated the request for a moment. He thought that it might be expedient to set the record straight and not to leave today's experiences to the public's interpretation.

'Yes, but you alone. Come in,' said Cardenzo.

When they were inside, Cardenzo explained to the girls that the water-well had been found and that human bones were buried there.

'Oh, good! Now the family will be happy and we can bury them with a nice ceremony,' said Candelaria.

'But they found hundreds of bones and do not know which belong to that family. We will have to wait until the bones can be identified and then have the burial ceremony,' said Cardenzo.

The reporter was trying to be patient, but was anxious to ask questions. He was busy writing his notes and did not want to miss the conversation because this was a new development, of which he had not been informed by Señor Guerra or any of the people near the well.

'Are you girls saying that the Spirits asked you to look for their remains in the well and, when you found them, to bury them again with a proper ceremony?' asked the reporter.

'Yes, that is what they asked us to do. They want to be buried in holy ground, otherwise they would not be at peace,' said Etna.

'Are you sure that's what they said to you?'

'Yes. We do not tell lies. Our Papa and Mama said that we must not tell lies,' said Etna.

'I don't mean to say that you are telling any lies. I just want to make sure that you remember what the Spirits said to you,' said the reporter.

'Tell the reporter what actually happened from the beginning, Etna,' said Cardenzo.

Etna related everything to the reporter and, in the few places where she may have omitted something, Candelaria was quick to correct her. The girls' encounters with the slave family were still fresh in their minds, and they related the story with great excitement.

'They must be buried in holy ground very soon. They have been waiting a long time to be at peace,' said Etna.

The reporter was moved by the girls' story and, although he was a sceptic about such things, he had to admit that their story was convincing and credible in the light of that day's events.

However, he wondered if there might be more to the girls' story of which they, themselves, were unaware. He could not tell the family what he was thinking. It was his interpretation of an external meaning to which he would have to give much further thought. But, so far as the girls were concerned, he considered their story and its revelations as an 'Unprecedented Happening' in the Valle.

As the reporter left, the crowd that had gathered outside the house was still demanding to speak to the girls. They said that they would not go away until they were told the full story of the girls' dreams.

The reporter was forced to speak to them. 'Please, everyone, you must go. You are distressing the girls by your insistence. Tomorrow morning, you will have the opportunity to read the girls' full story and my observations in the *Rebelde* newspaper, so please be good enough to leave.'

The crowd reluctantly drifted away, some of them insisting that they would return tomorrow and the following day to try to speak to the girls. Some of the people seemed to have issues of their own.

They may have had similar experiences and wanted them to be explained, or they may have thought that the girls might be able to enlighten them on their own problems. They may even have thought that the girls had acquired an ability to interpret supernatural events, and these people did not consider that the girls were merely caught up in a fracture of life that they could not explain.

The situation in the Valle was at risk of getting out of hand. In the present climate of the Cuban Revolution, a vociferous crowd would not normally gather in order to protest or to demand rights, concessions or privileges of any kind. That spelt danger for the demonstrators or for anyone allowing or encouraging them to do so, and this was the situation in which Señor Guerra was placed. He was in charge of the Manaca Estate and, if the crowd had continued to gather there too long, that would have had an adverse effect on its tourist business and he would have been held responsible.

He would also have been held responsible for allowing rumours about murders to circulate in the Valle and for enabling people to question the Socialism that the Government wanted to portray. If the security police had turned up at any time and arrested Señor Guerra, it would not have been a surprise to him or to some of the residents of the Valle. He was on dangerous ground.

The next day, as the reporter had promised, the story of the girls' dreams appeared on the front page of the *Rebelde* newspaper. The headline read: *'SPIRITS OF THE GRAVE SPOKE TO YOUNG GIRLS IN THE VALLE DE LOS INGENIOS'*.

The article began: *'There was alarm and consternation in the Valle de los Ingenios yesterday as two young sisters, Etna, aged 7, and Candelaria, aged 5, said that they were told by Spirits that their human remains lay buried in a disused water-well near the rail-track at the rear of the Iznaga Tower on the Manaca Estate.'*

The reporter, Señor Roberto Mendez, then went on to recount the full story of the girls' dreams and their ultimate consequences – the discovery of hundreds of human bones and the excitement caused by that discovery.

Señor Mendez continued: *'I believe that the girls are telling the truth about their encounters and conversations with these Spirits. Whether they were actual encounters or mere dreams is difficult to determine, but the subsequent discovery of human remains gives their story much credibility.*

I spoke to several spectators who had gathered at the scene and most of them seemed to have different opinions about what had taken place. Some said that it was the work of the Santeria which had cast a spell upon the girls. Others believed that the remains were of some of those who had lost their lives during certain battles of the Revolution. But the most outrageous suggestion was that put forward by an old man who had lived in the Valle for many years. He said that the remains were those of Martians who had landed in our island many years ago and been massacred by the unenlightened indigenous peoples.

I was not surprised to hear these types of comments, as our island is fraught with many inexplicable occurrences which we have come to accept as part of our culture. We have become so accustomed to hearing such stories that most of us do not take much notice of them any more. In most of these cases, the occurrences are not proven. Nevertheless, they all play a part in creating excitement, apprehension, fear of the unknown and even, sometimes, a change in the life style of those who believe them. We are a nation of believers in myths and superstitions and, especially when times are hard, we do not want to face reality and accept the occurrences for what they really are – fantasies.

Hence the spectators in the Valle failed to recognise that an 'Unprecedented Happening' had taken place. They were too ready to reflect on old beliefs and therefore closed their eyes to the fact that the Spirits had appeared to two innocent young girls who live sublime lives, not knowing any evil of the world. Their friends are their pet goat, cockerel and chicks with which they converse daily. The girls appear to be very happy in their environment, being on familiar terms with the wild birds and animals which they encounter every day – although that environment is a place of degradation, of spent blood and great anguish, a tarnished blot upon this part of our beloved land.

The spectators also failed to recognise that, if these girls had said that they had seen and spoken to the Virgin Mary, or the 'Mother of Charity', or to angels, they might have been worshipped and celebrated as saints. True revelations or prophecies or apparitions occur not only in the market place. They are found wherever Divine Providence dictates them to be and, in this case, the girls were the 'Appointed Ones' – innocent agents of an invisible and unexplainable supernatural hand.'

The reporter, Señor Mendez, should have stopped there, but he continued to give his own extended interpretation of events. He added: *'I believe that, so far as the 'Appointed Ones' are concerned, such 'occurrences' or 'happenings' may be the symptom of other underlying factors – such as a desire, wish, craving, hopeful expectation or some other psychological need which could not be expressed or explained in any other way. I can anticipate your question: "What are those desires or expectations?" I say, look around you. More precisely, look around where these girls live. I have been in their home and seen their way of life. I have observed their frugal existence – food and nourishment insufficient to sustain life or for healthy living, with only the necessities for survival, reminiscent of ancient times.*

The girls would have seen the comparative opulence displayed in the Manaca Mansion House – a symbol of good times. Subconsciously, they may have formed the impression that, if some people could live in such style – be they citizens of the Revolution or tourists – then why should they, who are in need, have to accept a status greatly short of that for which their fathers, brothers and sisters laid down their lives in the Revolution?

I am aware that we no longer suffer the hardships of the 'Special Period'. We survived through that difficult time in our lives and, since then, our country has made progress and developed even in spite of it. Today, I would not say that we are all suffering or living from hand to mouth, although we could do much better if certain embargoes which restrict our freedom of choice were removed. It is true that we do not suffer the poverty or deprivation of some other countries. We are healthy as a result of having an excellent health care system, and our enlightenment is assured by the availability of our free education system.

It must, however, be said that certain aspects of the Revolution have not achieved the aims, objects and standards of life that were prophesied by the advocates of the Revolution and by those who embarked on the 'Granma' on their journey to these shores. I am drawn to this conclusion by events such as the 'happenings' in the Valle de los Ingenios. Yet I have not heard a complaint from the Martinez girls or their family, nor from any of the other residents of the Valle. Their hardships are borne with fortitude and hope.

Nevertheless, the injustice was subconsciously declared by the girls who knew no other way to protest about their circumstances, except through the forces of their subconscious. As a result, their needs and desires were so great that they obliterated all traces of their impoverished state and all recognition of their harsh surroundings, leaving a vacuum in their brain waiting to be occupied by external and/or supernatural forces.'

This article by Señor Mendez was accompanied by several photographs of the Martinez family taken in their home and one photograph of the crowd which showed *'The Administrator, Señor Rafael Guerra, and Señor Virgilio Tomasas, a veteran guerrilla fighter of the Uprising"*.

The article caused consternation in the Government hierarchy, who did not see any merit in it. They saw only the negative side which detracted from the impression of the perfect State that the New Order wished to portray to its own people and the rest of the world, not least to the USA.

The Government appeared to have taken its eye off the ball. Its members may have been true revolutionaries, determined to achieve change and improve the lives of the people, but determination was not all that was needed to be successful. They needed the means to do so, and to put it into effect on an equal basis. Unfortunately they did not have the means – everything was in short supply and, for the system to work, the people had to undergo many sacrifices. So it worked on a precarious level of acceptance, having no alternative.

The article revealed the shortcomings of the State and disputed the impression it wanted to portray. Fidel had always boasted of the achievements of the Revolution but now, in the latter years of his life, he was being forced to address himself to the fact that the Revolution was not as successful as he would have wished. But there was no room for flexibility. His grip on the nation was too tight and his dealings with international matters too dogmatic.

Fidel may have also thought that, by the publication of this article, he could lose the pre-eminent position which he held internationally as a true and just revolutionary – especially among the peoples of Latin America, whose views were gradually changing from a docile acceptance of the Americans' point of view to one of their own nation's interests.

The Government may have considered shifting the blame to someone other than themselves. They were versed in influencing public opinion, and had many scapegoats to choose from – Señor Guerra being the obvious choice since he was in charge of the Valle de los Ingenios. They could have accused him of not carrying out the Government's instructions to improve the welfare of the Valle and, therefore, of being negligent in his duties. But, in this case, they could not safely do so since the people of the Valle knew that Señor Guerra was not given the resources by the Government to improve their lot, and whatever resources were given to him were to be used in the tourist business since that earned foreign currency for the Government.

The political state of affairs in the Valle seemed to be at fever pitch. Although the Regime had been in power for fifty years, criticisms of the Revolution were still not taken lightly. It seemed that Señor Mendez had forgotten this fact, having been absorbed or distracted by the 'happenings' in the Valle. He was accused of being a traitor, arrested and remanded to the *Isla de la Juventud* (the former

110

Isle of Pines) to await trial. The Editor of *Rebelde* was also suspended from his post for having failed in his duty to exercise due care and control of his reporters and to support the Revolution.

The Government then announced that they would send an official, Señor Alfonso Gomez, to investigate the 'happenings' in the Valle, with special emphasis on the Martinez family and other residents and their living conditions. Their aim was to rebut the assertions of the article by Señor Mendez, and to set an example by punishing him for misleading the people and being disloyal to the State. They were confident that Señor Gomez would find some evidence in the girls' story that would suit the policies and principles of the Revolution and maintain them in a good light.

Señor Alfonso Gomez was a big, strong man – both physically and politically. Before he became a Government trouble-shooter, he had worked in the Secret Service for several years, being responsible for the arrest of many of the dissidents who had tried to assassinate Fidel Castro and devised other plots to destabilise the country. His policy was to 'punish the disloyal and execute the traitor'. He was, therefore, well-respected by the Government and chosen as the man to get to the bottom of the problem in the Valle.

Several weeks later, the Forensic Pathologist's Department returned the excavated remains to Señor Guerra, together with its report. That said that tests had identified 355 entities. Of those, 350 were Amerindian Indians – more specifically, of the Taino tribe – while 5 entities were of African genes. The forensic tests indicated that the Amerindians must have been massacred, for there were multiple abrasions, wounds and even decapitations, which showed a large degree of violence. The report stated that a massacre must have taken place around 1750 to 1760, but it did not make any allegations as to who was responsible for the massacre or its circumstances.

The report further stated that the African genes were of five people from the mainland of West Africa, probably from Gambia or Guinea. There were three adults – two male and one female, and two young persons – one male and one female, all with shared genes. They had several bullet wounds and it appeared that was the main cause of their death. The report assessed the deaths to have taken place around 1870 to 1875 and suggested that they may have been a

111

family of slaves, but could not say who might have been responsible or the circumstances of their death.

The full report was published in *Rebelde*, with no additional comments except to remind the people that a Government investigation was in progress. Now that the Investigator, Señor Gomez, was aware of the forensic report, which confirmed the origins of the remains, it was only left for him to determine the truth or falsity of the incidents surrounding the girls' story and their living conditions.

The forensic report did not go unnoticed by the people of the Valle. They began to hail the girls as having extra-sensory perception or some special antennae or ability to receive signals from beyond the grave. Many people turned up outside the Martinez home demanding that the girls communicate with their dead relatives or decipher their dreams. The more puritan of the crowd turned up at the Manaca Mansion House and demanded that all the remains found in the water-well must now be interred in 'holy ground' as was requested of the girls by the Spirits.

Señor Guerra addressed the crowd and told them that it had always been his intention, since the discovery of the remains, to rebury them in 'holy ground', but now that there was a Government investigation into these matters, he would have to wait until its completion. The crowd could not argue against such an explanation. To do so would have placed them at risk of being accused of disloyalty to the authority of the Government. They would therefore have to wait until the Government investigation was completed.

The Investigator, Señor Alfonso Gomez, decided to concentrate on the main issue that could reflect badly on the Government – its alleged negligence to provide for a reasonable standard of living for the people of the Valle, especially the Martinez family. He thought that the girls' parents had put them up to deceive the public about their hard life and therefore force the Government to improve their lives by favouring them over other residents in the Valle.

Señor Gomez believed that the facts and the truth could easily be ascertained by questioning Etna and Candelaria who were not old enough to understand his strategy and interrogation skills. He first had to prove that the girls' dreams were a pack of lies and, once that was established, it would follow that the report in the *Rebelde* newspaper by Señor Roberto Mendez had no foundation whatsoever.

Señor Gomez's manner towards the girls was very severe. He believed that, in this way, he would force the truth out of them and make them confess that they were put up to it. Cardenzo and Amelia were asked to wait in another room while he conducted the interrogation.

'Now that your parents are not here, you can tell me the truth. You did not really have those dreams about the African slaves, did you?'

'We did, Señor, and we told Mama and Papa,' said Candelaria.

'It is true, Señor. They even told us where their bones could be found,' said Etna.

'Your Mama and Papa told you the story about the slaves, didn't they?'

'No, Señor, we saw the slaves ourselves and they told us to look in the water-well near the rail-track. We told Mama and Papa what they had told us,' said Etna.

'I believe that you are not telling the truth because you cannot see things which do not exist,' said Señor Gomez.

'But we saw them in our dreams. They were real to us, Señor,' said Etna.

'If I tell you that your neighbours also do not believe you and they said that you are not telling the truth, would you admit now that that is so?'

'Our neighbours would not say those things, Señor. They know that we always tell the truth because Mama and Papa have always told us to do so,' said Etna.

'I must tell you that if you do not change your story, your Mama and Papa will be taken away from you and you will not see them again.'

'Where will you take them, Señor?' asked Candelaria.

'To prison, in a far away place, where they would be punished and would be unhappy,' said Señor Gomez.

'Would we and our friends be able to visit them?' asked Candelaria.

'Neither you nor your friends would be able to visit them in prison,' said Señor Gomez.

'Are there windows in prison?' asked Etna.

'Yes, with iron bars so that your Mama and Papa could not escape.'

'But you would not be able to prevent our friends from entering through the windows to visit Mama and Papa,' said Etna.

'Who are these 'friends' you speak about?'

'Our chicks and all the birds in the Valle. We will tell them that our Mama and Papa are in prison and they would want to go and visit them,' said Etna.

'And Dulcina and Gallina,' said Candelaria. 'And they would be sad because they know that it is our Mama and Papa who allow us to feed them, Señor.'

'Do you feed your 'friends' every day?' asked Señor Gomez.

'Yes, Señor. Mama and Papa always give us food to feed them,' said Etna.

'But they are always hungry and want more, especially Dulcina,' said Candelaria.

'Now, tell me, does your Mama give you food to eat every day?' asked Señor Gomez.

'Yes, Señor,' said Etna.

'What does she give you to eat?'

'One day she gives us a piece of her baked bread and butter. The next day we may get a papaya fruit,' said Etna.

'Is that for breakfast or lunch?' asked Señor Gomez.

'For breakfast, Señor,' said Candelaria.

'We don't have lunch, Señor,' said Etna.

'And what do they give you for dinner?'

'Sometimes one slice of meatloaf or a meat ball from Mama and Papa's weekly rations,' said Etna.

'And are you happy with that? Do you still feel hungry?'

'We are quite happy, Señor. We have not been eating very much since we were born,' said Etna. 'Mama and Papa do not eat very much either. They say that we must be happy for whatever little we have and be thankful that we are free to speak to our friends and to have our Mama and Papa with us.

'So if you take Mama and Papa to prison who is going to feed our friends and us, Señor?' exclaimed Candelaria.

'Do your Papa and Mama ever speak about the Revolution?' asked Señor Gomez.

'Yes, Señor,' said Etna.

'What do they say about it?'

'They say that they are in this Valle working for the Revolution, and when it is successful we will all have a better life,' said Etna.

'And we will return to our little farm in Camaguey where Papa and his family were very happy,' said Candelaria.

'Are your Mama and Papa happy in this Valle?' asked Señor Gomez.

'Yes, Señor. They are happy because they have us,' said Etna.

'And Grandma too, Etna,' said Candelaria.

'Are you telling the truth when you say that your Mama and Papa, or anyone else, did not tell you about the dreams?'

'Yes, Señor,' said Candelaria.

'Do you have children, Señor?' asked Etna.

'Yes, I have two sons and two daughters. They are grown up now.'

'And when they were little like us, did they tell lies to you?' asked Etna.

'Yes, sometimes.'

'Why didn't you teach them not to tell lies, Señor?' asked Etna.

Señor Gomez hesitated.

'Did they love you, Señor?' asked Candelaria.

'Oh yes, they did and still do.'

'But, for them to love you, Señor, did you speak to them as angry as you speak to us?' asked Etna.

'What do you mean?' asked Señor Gomez.

'You seem to be unhappy, Señor. You raise your voice in anger even though we tell you the truth about our dreams. We do not speak to the birds and the animals like that. We are gentle to them and, in return, they are not afraid of us. We speak to them and they speak to us in their own way,' said Etna.

'You speak to the birds and animals? Can I see you speaking to the birds and animals – as you say, your 'friends?' asked Señor Gomez.

Etna and Candelaria led him out to the backyard to visit Dulcina, the chicks and Gallina, and to be introduced to them.

'This is Señor Gomez from the Government. He wants to meet you,' said Etna.

'And he is very unhappy because he does not have his children any more to love him,' said Candelaria.

'This is Dulcina. Say 'Hello' to Señor Gomez, Dulcina,' said Etna. Ignoring Señor Gomez, Dulcina suggested that he was disappointed because they had not come to feed him.

'And this is Gallina. She gives us milk and is very friendly. Say 'Hello' to Señor Gomez, Gallina,' said Candelaria. Gallina also ignored Señor Gomez and did not show her teeth in appreciation of the introduction. The chicks too were quiet, as if they sensed an intruder in their midst.

'They think that you are unhappy and do not like them, Señor,' said Etna.

'But I do like birds and animals,' protested Señor Gomez.

'They think that you are a bad man, Señor,' said Candelaria.

'They also know that you are angry and unhappy. They know what is in your heart, and that is why they are not happy to meet you,' said Etna.

'Why do you say that I am unhappy?' asked Señor Gomez.

'We know it, Señor, and Dulcina and Gallina know it as well,' said Etna.

Señor Gomez realised that he was dealing with two girls possessed of the highest sensitivity to detect any feeling of belligerence and anger in his soul. He was amazed, and wondered if the girls could read his mind and, therefore, know what his work entailed and the degree of sorrow that he had brought to many families who were unjustly accused as traitors of the Revolution.

Señor Gomez was known as the 'Iron Man', and he may have believed that his cloak of iron could protect him from detection by his enemies or anyone who wanted to know his thoughts or his way of life. But every man who is engaged in such activities as his should

116

realise that he radiates an aura of personal self that only the highly sensitive or persons possessed of a 'Seventh Sense', such as the girls, could detect.

This realisation alarmed him and made him uncomfortable. He felt that, instead of him interrogating the girls, it was they who were analysing him – not deliberately, but naturally and innocently, because of the simplicity of their minds and the way in which they saw the Valle and the world.

Señor Gomez did not realise it, but as his interrogation continued, the harshness of his tone had gradually disappeared and his questions and responses were milder, which had now turned his interrogation into a polite conversation. There was something going on with these two girls which he could not definitely put his finger on – their manner, assumptions and innocence, and their simplicity, which appeared to him to be so extraordinary. He had never experienced that before, not when he himself was a young boy, born just before the Revolution, and not even in the character of his own children.

The 'Iron Man' of the Security Services had tried his best to disprove the girls' account of their dreams but had to admit defeat. How could he not believe these girls who accepted their hardships as normal and lived life as if they were living in Paradise?

Señor Gomez concluded in his mind that there was no evidence or hint of a fabricated story. The girls' story may have been an unusual one – believable or unbelievable – but there was no deception here. He came to believe that the girls were incapable of that. In all his years as an interrogator of crimes and deception, he had never seen or experienced the innocence and consistency of their answers and thought processes. The girls had made him look inwardly at his own life and to re-examine his attitude to others – acknowledging that not everyone is a criminal because an accusation is made, and that there are certain things in life which humans possess, such as dignity and a natural sense of truth and honesty. These things he had found in the girls. He therefore decided that there was no need to investigate further.

As it turned out, the public did not have long to wait. Señor Gomez could be said to have completed his task in record time. It appeared that he may also have been under instructions to bring the matter to a rapid conclusion, so as to prevent too much speculation and to avoid the public dwelling on any shortcomings of the Government, should he find any evidence to that effect.

The Investigator declared that all that had been reported by Señor Roberto Mendez in the *Rebelde* newspaper was correct. He said he thought that the Martinez family and other families in the Valle were far from being beneficiaries of the advantages of the Revolution. Although this result was not the intention of the Government, these families had, through some oversight, escaped the safety net and fallen into deprivation. He said that the most hopeful sign of life that existed in the Valle was the sincerity of the two girls, Etna and Candelaria, and the fertility that grows the sugar-cane – but man cannot live on the juice of the sugar-cane alone. The 'Iron Man', it seemed, had begun to melt.

After the report by Señor Gomez was published, the people started to protest in support of the *Rebelde* reporter, Señor Roberto Mendez, and his Editor. The Government came to realise that it had acted irrationally in making the arrest. In order to avoid civil unrest and to appear benevolent and reasonable, Señor Mendez was released from custody and the Editor was reinstated in his post. The Government also ordered that all the excavated remains be interred as requested by the two girls and the Martinez family.

The people, however, wanted more. They also demanded the reinstatement of Señor Mendez whom they claimed was a truthful and loyal son of the Revolution, and whose father had fought with the rebels against Batista for a better life. They argued that one of the advantages of that better life was a good education, where one is taught to use his intelligence and to make the best use of his abilities. The Government decided it would be expedient to reinstate Señor Roberto Mendez as a reporter with the *Rebelde* newspaper.

Although the Cuban people were actively encouraged to protest against foreign injustices, such as the long-running cases of the 'Miami Five' (accused of spying in the US) or Elian Gonzalez (the young Cuban boy caught up in a custody dispute), protest against their own Government or anything connected to local matters was unheard of, and would almost certainly carry the risk of imprisonment or deportation.

To a large extent, any demonstrations were successfully controlled. The Government would know of any dissent long before it got out of hand, thanks to the Local Committee system and informers. It is noted that the people of the Valle did not protest about the unequal system that existed there, even though such a protest would have been more justified and for their mutual benefit. In effect, people were afraid that if they did so it would have been considered a direct attack upon the policies of the Government, and there would have been severe punishment meted out. Protesting for justice for others was thought of as a safer activity where the whole community was involved, making it more difficult for individual protestors to be held accountable. It seems to be the assumption of revolutionaries that Revolutions generally are carried out for the greater benefit of the people, and that it does not matter whether the measures taken to achieve that benefit are reasonable, humane or approved by the majority of the people.

CHAPTER TEN

INTERMENT

A few weeks later, the people gathered in the Valle. A large crowd came to witness the funeral ceremonies for the African family and the Amerindian Indians in the local cemetery which was on consecrated holy ground. They were there to pay homage to souls which had been lost but then were found – souls that had laboured in the Valle and been forced to learn a new way of life much different from their own, where the strain of humanity did not exist in the hearts of men.

A cool breeze blew over the congregation and the sky became populated by a flock of birds, while the 'green lakes' of sugar-cane swayed in the fields as though waving a final '*Adios*' to those long-lost souls who will always be remembered as comrades in the fight for survival – survival of the plough and the bullet, a universal and everlasting survival.

Among those in attendance were the Minister of the Interior, the Ambassadors of Gambia and Guinea, Señor Alfonso Gomez (the Government Investigator), Señor Roberto Mendez and the Editor of *Rebelde*, Señor Guerra, and almost all the residents of the Valle, including Señor and Señora Bronski. Señor Tomasas was invited but did not attend. The guests of honour were, of course, Etna and Candelaria and the Martinez family.

Representatives of Gambian and Guinean religious communities performed the rites over their brethren, and Elders and spokesmen for the Amerindian Indians conducted their ceremonies in an atmosphere of solemnity. The bones of the five entities which constituted the African family were buried together in a joint grave, while those of the Amerindians were all grouped together and buried in a single mass grave. After the prayers, and when all the remains had been lowered into the holy ground, a minute's silence was observed before the drums rolled in lament for them. At last, they were at the end of their restless wanderings – 130 years in the case of the African family, and 250 years for the Amerindians. One wondered whether they would have agreed with Hatuey's words: 'If there are Spaniards in Heaven, I would rather be in Hell'. They had been in Hell for over 200 years, and now they had finally been given release from that place.

Cardenzo wanted to make a speech before the ceremony had ended, but he was advised against doing so by Etna and Candelaria. They told him that was not what the African family or the Amerindians would have wanted. They did not want recrimination, for their murderers would have already received their punishment long ago. The girls seemed to have a deeper intuition of their feelings – their 'Seventh Sense' that made them truly cognizant of the wishes of those who had died.

This gathering in the Valle could never have been conceived in the minds of the people or the Government. It was most unusual. Two young girls who had no experience of life and who had no family or any other connection with the deceased had been the instruments of their 'resurrection'.

The Government could not defeat innocence, and the magnitude of an important event could even be achieved indirectly by that innocence. In the course of life, some stand out from the crowd above all others because they are different in ways which make them shine, and they are recognised by the people as exceptional human beings although the reasons for their light are not always understood. One could call this phenomenon 'superstition', 'miracles', 'magic', 'genius' or 'apparitions, supernatural or divine', but call it what you may, it suggests that there are forces beyond our control or understanding in the world in which we live. In the Valle, this innocence triggered off a series of events which were conjured up from the dreams of two young girls, and the people did not only 'believe' but were able to see for themselves the results of their claims.

After the funeral, everyone who attended walked slowly away – contemplative of the day's proceedings. They walked behind the Martinez family and looked at Etna and Candelaria in a fresh light, expectant that they would lead the way again in the future. They wondered what new revelations the girls would disclose – revelations, whether imagined or perceived, that only they could bring to light because they had that special insight or special relationship with the unknown. But they were still young girls, and it would be many years before they would make their mark and again bring the Valle to the attention of the public.

CHAPTER ELEVEN

PROPHECIES

That night Etna and Candelaria went to bed early, exhausted by all the excitement of the day. They were happy knowing that they had kept their promise to the African family and now they could sleep uninterrupted and in peace.

But try as they might, the 'Appointed Ones' could not sleep. Their minds were disturbed by uncertainties. Had they fulfilled their promise? Did they achieve what was expected of them? Would the African family, and also the Amerindians, be pleased? They pondered for some time. But young minds need rest, and they eventually fell asleep and did not expect to wake again until they heard the crowing of Dulcina the next morning.

In the early hours of the morning, they heard, instead, the faint percussions of distant drums and the sounds of a hollowed horn and a bell. They awoke in a glow of sparkling light as though glittering in the reflection of the stars. Five images revealed themselves – all dressed in splendid robes of gold and diamonds. They were the African family, now transformed as figures of opulence and majesty, as though they were visiting royalty with their entourage in attendance upon them. The pain and suffering which previously permeated them had now vanished from their countenance.

'Do not be alarmed, my angels, we are your friends and guardians. We are here again to thank you both for rescuing us and restoring the lustre in our souls, and for bringing peace in the land of our fathers. We are released from Limbo where uncalled spirits occupy vacant space,' said Grandfather Abufera.

'You look beautiful and magnificent,' said Etna.

'Yes, you look lovely,' said Candelaria.

'We are in our rightful place now, thanks to you. Before our enforced transportation to this foreign land, we were granted royal status by the Mightiest of our Fathers.'

'How did you come to our country?' asked Etna.

'One day, in our own country, we were out walking in the forest in search of our friend the proud lion, the king of beasts. Those were joyful days when we had freedom of the wilderness. We knew the fiercest animals by name and we all lived in harmony. We knew no strangers then and had no fear that they would appear and rob us of our freedom. We were captured and taken to a ship where we joined a multitude of our people, chained and stained with blood and in putrid conditions to which we were unaccustomed. The black ocean raged in anger at our treatment. It washed some of our people overboard and relieved them of their sorrows. By grace of fortune we reached your land, where we were humiliated and sold in cattle auctions and died in slavery. That was many years ago,' said Abufera.

'We are sorry….,' said Etna.

'Do not be sorry, my angels. It was not your doing, but that of men of minds who thought their lives would last forever, that happiness was found in the suppression of others, and that they would enjoy the fruits of their plunder. Little did they know that life is but an instant of time and they would perish in agony for the evils of their souls and not by hand of mortal flesh,' said Abufera. 'My grandson and my granddaughter want to say a few words to you.'

'We thank you with all our hearts for releasing us from our past life where we lived in a world of never-ending darkness,' said Tatantumbo.

'So dark that not even the eyes could see, except through the senses,' added Claratuma.

'It was only when our senses came into contact with you that the light was shown in our eyes again,' said Tatantumbo.

'Are you happy now?' asked Candelaria.

'Yes, thanks to you, we will be forever happy, for there is no place more beautiful than where we are now and the memory of our pains has vanished. When we were slaves, we did not live the life of children. We were thought not fit for learning. We were kept ignorant of the world and our homeland was banished from our minds. We were deprived of the pleasures of childhood – the natural things of youth, the things children expect when growing up, and the joys of the natural world – like your friendship with the animals. We did not have that pleasure. Even the birds and animals kept their distance, for what they saw might have shocked them and imposed a restriction on their freedom,' said Tatantumbo.

'Is this beautiful place across the sea?' asked Etna.

'It is across the seas and oceans and plains, and beyond the world as you know it. It is a place beyond space and time, inconceivable even to your imagination,' said Tatantumbo.

'Could we go there some day?' asked Candelaria.

'Yes, after you have lived many years. Your place is already reserved for you – but only after you have fulfilled your destiny and when your energies can achieve no more,' said Tatantumbo.

'Are you still ignorant of the world?' asked Etna.

'It is very perceptive of you to ask such a question. We are no longer ignorant. We are now blessed with all the wisdom of the ages, and we see the dark side of men and know that they have a long way to go before they enter the 'Road to Perfection' and the 'Avenue of the Divine',' said Claratuma.

'Will our Mama and Papa always be with us?' asked Candelaria.

'Your Mama and Papa will always be with you. Your relationship will never end, for the chain of blood is never broken. That is as much as we are allowed to say to guide you to the 'Road to Perfection',' said Claratuma.

'Were you pleased with the funeral ceremony?' asked Etna.

'You did us proud for ones so young but well versed with nature and having the conscience and wisdom of many. You believed in our plight, in our prayers and our appeal for release from the chains that bound us and deprived us of our rightful place. You showed understanding more knowledgeable than elders who claim renown. We are ever beholden to you and, in our prayers, you will always be with us,' said Abufera.

'Will we see you again?' asked Candelaria.

'We have all agreed that would be our pleasure, but now we are in the hands of the Almighty One – the Lord of all mankind who controls our destiny – where all worthy souls go to rest until called upon for service in His cause. Should we be selected to serve mankind, we will be with you again at that time,' said Abufera.

'I am sad that we may never meet again,' said Etna

'Do not be sad, my angels, for we see your future upon this earth, bright and free from present hardships, the sea constant in your lives, 'natural friends' in harmony with your thoughts, enjoying your childhood until the time comes to enter into your adult lives. When you see the *cangrejos* begin to cross the danger zone before their time, a new era will have begun. Out of oblivion, a man of race will ascend, fulfilling the prophecies of our Ancient Sages. New roots of reconciliation will begin to bloom, and peace will reign in the Western Hemisphere. Years will pass before the *cangrejos* retrace their steps and dangers fight to reign.

So we say to you, do not be alarmed if you see the bright clouds turn dark, icicles fall as rain in the hot sun, rivers freeze over and turn into ice, hurricanes visit more often than the seasons would presently permit, and if strange languages beyond your comprehension are heard in your land.'

'When will that happen?' asked Etna.

'Perhaps not in your lifetime, but in time to come,' said Abufera.

'But will we be happy with our Mama and Papa tomorrow?' asked Etna.

'You will be happy all the days of your life. But you must know the true meaning of happiness. It is not personal enjoyment or self-gratification or wealth. It is the service that you provide to others who are in need, your consideration and support in times of hardship, the possession of pure thoughts – all given with an honest heart, although no benefit or reward is received or expected. Where we are now, happiness is measured in different terms than how your world knows it. So bear your sorrows magnificently, and let the tears which may flow cleanse your eyes that you may see life is but a passing phase on the way to eternity.

Now, farewell my angels, and "*Adios*" in your tongue! I hope that we will meet again,' said Abufera.

The next day, the girls told their parents about their 'dream' in which the African family had reappeared – this time as royals, dressed in fine clothes and jewels. When their parents heard that, they thought their daughters were truly blessed. But this time, although they believed the girls' dream, they told them to keep it to themselves and not to tell anyone. Cardenzo and Amelia were afraid for the welfare of their daughters, as a crowd still gathered outside demanding their advice as though in need of a physician.

CPSIA information can be obtained
at www.ICGtesting.com
Printed in the USA
LVHW021337100521
686964LV00013B/952